REAPING

Angels

LAURA THALASSA

BURNING EMBER PRESS

CHAPTER 1

Angel

HAD I KNOWN I was going to face down death today, I totally would've bought myself the Slurpee.

Instead, I walked out of the convenience store with a single packet of mints and a magazine. I touched the homeless man who lingered outside. His bloodshot eyes cleared a bit, that too-bright edge to them dimming to a more normal sheen.

I ignored the onlookers who snapped photos of me from their smartphones and headed for my white Mustang.

My cleavage buzzed. A second later, "*Bad boys bad boys, whatcha gonna do, whatcha gonna do when they come for you ...*"

I groaned. Perfect timing for a call from the L.A.P.D.

They were the sister organization to the Los Angeles *Supernatural* Department, or L.A.S.D., which I was a part of, and we often teamed up to fight crime in southern California.

I reached down the front of my gold jumpsuit, noticing that even more people had stopped to take pictures while I fished the device out. I waved at them and smiled.

Really needed to invest in pockets.

"Hey Ramirez," I said, lifting the phone to my ear as I hopped into my car, "thought you lost your phone."

"He found it," said an unfamiliar voice. "Bottom of his locker. This is Officer Jensen. Ramirez told me to call you on his behalf." I'd never heard of Officer Jensen. Had Ramirez gotten a new partner without telling me?

"Why isn't he calling me himself?"

"He's talking to the fire department at the moment."

Shit. I gripped my phone tighter. The police and the fire department in one location? Something happened.

"What's going on?" I asked.

"An electrical fire broke out at the K-12 Reading Center in South Central, just off of Slauson Avenue."

My stomach bottomed out. "What?"

"Know the place?" he asked, hearing the tone of my voice.

"Yeah, I do." I went to the Reading Center during my free time and hung out with the at-risk kids.

I rubbed my eyes. "How bad is it?"

"Bad. Firefighters haven't been able to get inside. Place is locked up, windows are barred."

My palms were already beginning to sweat. Not the kids. I hated emergencies with kids. "How many are trapped inside?"

"Don't know. We think two to three dozen."

"M'kay, I'm on it."

I started up the engine and flipped on my siren.

Move the hell out of the way people, I've got some kids to save.

I SCREECHED TO a halt behind the fire trucks and ambulances that surrounded the burning building. Just beyond them the area had been cordoned off.

I slammed the car door shut and approached the nearest officer. I didn't need to pull out a badge; they knew who I was by my outfit alone.

"Angel, just the woman I wanted to see."

"What's going on?" I asked. "Has anyone been able to get inside yet?"

"No. We've been working on the door, but the thing's built like Fort Knox."

Not surprising given the area. The Learning Center would get robbed blind in this neighborhood without the extra security measures. My eyes cut to the door. A fireman wielding an axe swung at the knob. As I watched, the handle snapped off, and he kicked the door open.

I pushed past the officer and charged after the fireman, steeling myself for the heat.

I fucking hate getting singed.

I stepped through the flames, only pausing on the other side of the entrance.

That ... didn't hurt.

I blinked, glancing down at my bodysuit. It still shone a burnished gold. My exposed skin remained unblemished.

"Well, I'll be damned."

I squinted at the hallway in front of me. The fireman who ran in here before me was nowhere in sight. My skin prickled as an eerie silence replaced the roar of the flames.

Behind me the door slammed shut.

I swiveled around, and the first thing I noticed was that it was not the door to the Reading Center. That door currently had handprint turkeys plastered across it.

The second thing I noticed was the building's unblemished interior. The flames that had risen into the sky hadn't scorched the walls, or the floor, or the ceiling. In fact, now that I was inside, the fire had disappeared altogether, as though it had never existed in the first place.

"Fuck me."

I'd walked right into a trap.

CHAPTER 2

Angel

JUST FOR THE hell of it, I tried the doorknob. Locked. Big surprise.

I rotated to face the rest of the building. It *appeared* abandoned, but I knew better.

I strode down the hall, poking my head into the empty office rooms I came upon. Old furniture and tagged walls greeted me. Wherever I was, it wasn't the Reading Center.

What kind of super could weave an illusion this powerful? And why would they target me? I was a medic; all I did was heal the wounded.

As I continued down the corridor, the hair on my arms stood on end. Someone hidden watched me.

I halted.

"I know you're there," I said. "You might as well show yourself."

A thud sounded behind me as that someone dropped to their feet.

I turned, and when my eyes fell on my assailant, I sucked in a breath of air.

"Ah crap."

For every superhero, there was a supervillain. Standing in front of me was one of the worst of them, the Executioner, the killer of superheroes.

Imposingly tall and clad all in black, he was L.A.S.D.'s boogeyman, someone I'd hoped to never cross. He was the Cruel Countess's right hand man, and supposedly responsible for dozens of superhero disappearances over the last two years.

My eyes moved from the leather hood that covered half his face to the gloves he wore. My pulse picked up as I stared at those gloves, knowing what lay beneath. Charred bodies. Twisted faces. He burned people alive with his touch.

"What do you want with me?" I fought the urge to back up. I was a superhero, damn it!

The corner of the Executioner's wicked mouth lifted. "Your cooperation."

I steeled myself. "Doubt that's going to happen."

The Executioner sauntered towards me, the leather straining over his muscles. "Perhaps you need a little convincing."

For every one of his steps forward I took one back, until I bumped the far wall of the building. My escape lay on the other end of the hallway, and I'd need to outmaneuver him to get there.

I followed him with my eyes and tried to ignore the fact that I was probably going to die today.

"So the fire ... ?"

The Executioner took another step forward. "An illusion."

"And Officer Jensen?" Another step.

"Not real."

Now I know who stole Ramirez's phone.

"That's a pretty elaborate set up for one little superhero."

He stopped in front of me. "Don't sell yourself short. If you weren't powerful, I wouldn't be here."

My heart rate escalated. "Why *are* you here?"

"The Cruel Countess has use of you."

So the Cruel Countess was involved with this. Shit.

If I agreed, would I find out where the missing superheroes were, or would I simply become one of them?

Tread carefully, Angel.

"Where would we be going?" I asked.

"Away. If you come quietly, you can save yourself torture."

Don't look at the door, don't look at the door.

If I chanced a glance, he'd know I was trying to figure a way past him. Curious as I was to find the missing superheroes and see what the Cruel Countess planned for them, I wasn't going anywhere with him.

The Executioner held out a gloved hand. "This doesn't have to be hard."

But it did.

I brought up a boot and kicked him in the chest. The move wasn't very powerful or all that well placed, but the fucker was surprised, and really, that was all that counted.

He stumbled back and, sidestepping him, I sprinted for the door. Dipping a hand down my top, I fished for my cellphone, which was once again nestled in my cleavage. I seriously needed pockets.

I pushed my legs harder while I pulled the device out. I would live through this. I'd be the exception.

The Executioner plowed into me from behind, his arms wrapping around my waist. He tackled me to the ground. The phone flew from my hand and skittered down the hall as my jaw cracked against the floor.

Well, there went *that* plan.

Pushing me onto my back, the supervillain straddled my torso. He gritted his teeth and yanked my wrists above my head.

"Care to reconsider, Angel?" He stared down at me, and I could see his eyes glint from the shadows.

"Get off of me." I twisted against him, struggling to free myself. He might as well have been made of metal.

"Not an answer."

The Executioner pulled off a glove with his teeth. I eyed the bare skin like it was a venomous snake and bucked against him.

"Last chance to do this the easy way," he said, his voice deep.

I thrashed under the weight of his body, but he was simply too big and me too small.

My heart beat madly as his hand crept closer. He drew out the action, probably believing that fear would make me reevaluate his offer.

I lifted my chin and squared my jaw. "Screw. You."

Warm skin caressed the nape of my neck. The Executioner's hands were surprisingly gentle for a seasoned torturer. My eyes moved to his face, cloaked in the shadow of his hood. A long moment went by.

And then another. And another.

I blinked. The skin should've bubbled and blistered, my insides should've been lit on fire. Instead, only the soothing warmth of the Executioner's body heat seeped into mine.

It wasn't working. The fiercest villain in the entire world had come here to break me, and he couldn't.

Harry Potter ain't got nothing on me, bitches.

At some point, the Executioner also realized it wasn't working. He removed his grip from my neck and stared at his hand. "It didn't hurt you," he said, stunned.

He reached out once more.

Oh come on.

For a second time his deadly hand touched the skin of my neck. There it rested.

I'd seen photos of his victims. The bad ones were nothing more than charcoal, roasted from the inside out. Those that held on a little longer ... they could cling to an agonizing existence for something like a week before they finally succumbed to the burns.

The Executioner and I stared at each other. My heart beat steadily, and other than being crushed under a huge dude, my breathing was stable.

Still wasn't working.

You would've thought someone had hit the man upside the head, he looked so stunned.

Rather than removing his hand, the Executioner began *stroking* the skin of my neck. His touch was cautious, almost … wondrous. His hand glided up my neck to my jaw and his thumb grazed my lower lip. I heard his breathing hitch and felt his body shudder.

I swallowed. Quiz me this: what would a man want to do with the first woman he couldn't willfully burn?

He lifted his hand long enough to pull back his hood.

I sucked in a breath of air as I got my first good look at the supervillain.

The Executioner was *hot*. No, *hot* didn't begin to cover it. He was come-in-my-pants beautiful.

And of course, he had to be evil. *Why do all the sexy guys have to have issues? Why?*

Strands of nearly black hair swept back from his face. Deep, dark eyes gazed back at me.

He leaned in, so close I could feel his cool breath against my skin. His hand went to my cheek, his fingers trailing over the skin there. His expression was full of wonder. Oh, and lust. A crapload of lust was there as well. He glanced down at my mouth.

"Don't," I warned him.

He smiled. And then his lips met mine.

CHAPTER 3

Executioner

SHE CAN ENDURE my touch!

No one had before—not completely. Not my father, not all the hits I'd made in the years between then and now. Were all healers immune to the ravages of my ability? I'd never considered it. *Why* had I never considered it?

Sure my skin had grazed others without hurting them too badly; there'd even been other women. Debasing acts done in the dark and me sweating with the effort of holding back my punishing power. But not until today had I met someone who could neutralize that power in its entirety.

And my God, this woman tasted like heaven.

How long I have waited for this.

Her lips were softer than I'd imagined, but even that contact couldn't satiate my hunger. My fingers skimmed along Angel's jaw again, reveling in the feel of her skin.

The Fates had finally delivered me a woman. Just when I'd been sure they'd turned their backs on me, too.

My mouth continued its languid perusal of hers. Countless times I'd hoped for this ... normality. Hoped until the wanting nearly crushed me. At some point I'd had to stop.

But now ... now those hopes came rushing back to the surface.

The Cruel Countess would have to find another superhero to take Angel's place. There was no way I was giving this woman up.

Now that I'd found her, she was mine.

Angel

THE EXECUTIONER WAS a good kisser. Really good. So good that, in a moment of weakness, I *might* have kissed him back.

His tongue caressed mine, and I made a small, satisfied sound. Damn me and my traitorous mouth; I was being seduced by a very handsome, very dangerous man.

His hand brushed down my body, and the spell was broken.

The Executioner tried to roast me alive, and now I was making out with him.

Hell no.

Only, he still held my hands in place. I wasn't getting away from him unless I got creative.

I smothered my rising anger; that wouldn't do me any good at the moment. No, this called for trickery.

Pinching my eyes shut, I pressed myself against him. Just as I suspected, the Executioner's strength was also his weakness. He wanted to touch everything.

He let my wrists go to run his hands over my torso. The moment he did so, I fisted my hand and swung. The right hook landed exactly where I wanted it to—his temple.

The Executioner swayed, and I pushed him off me so I could scramble away.

Not fast enough.

His hand shot out and latched onto my ankle. I pulled my other leg back and kicked him in the crotch. "That's what I think about your offer, asshole."

The Executioner let me go to clutch himself. He groaned. "You ... play ... dirty."

"Oh, like you're one to talk." I picked up my phone where it had fallen. The captain would know what to do.

"Get the hell out of there."

"Wait, seriously?" My captain wanted me to ... run? From danger?

"Do you really want to take on the Executioner? Tonight?"

I turned further away from my villain-turned-victim. "I just did."

"The man is wanted in twenty-seven different countries.

Nations that can't even agree on basic human rights agree that the Executioner needs to be stopped. You're great at what you do, Angel, but I'm afraid that someone with your abilities won't be able to take him down by yourself."

I clenched the phone in my hands. *Someone with my abilities.* As if I couldn't also kick ass and take names. As if being a healer and being a weakling were synonymous.

"You know what?" I said, turning to face the Executioner, "I will bring him—aw damn."

The Executioner was gone.

CHAPTER 4

Angel

THE CRUEL COUNTESS's henchman was in town, and he was after me. I clenched the steering wheel tighter and worried my lower lip.

I was immune to his power. Was there any precedent for this?

It made sense. I healed with my touch. He injured with his.

I clicked on the car's police radio for any nearby shootings. Now was one of the rare times the radio had fallen silent. Just when I needed a good fix too. Some people are addicted to coffee, others alcohol, others gambling. My power was my addiction.

Unconsciously, I began steering my car in the direction

of the nearest hospital.

Shouldn't be doing this. I'd made a promise to myself to only heal in the line of duty. Too many miracles affected the balance of life and death. Yet here I was, considering it—again—and not even because I was such a damn softie. Nope. The Executioner had whittled me down to a junkie hankering for my next fix.

I survived the Executioner.

I suppressed a shudder. Today would not be the last day I saw that man. Not after that kiss and the possessive look in his eyes. Nope, he'd be coming back for more, and not just on behalf of the Cruel Countess.

It appeared I'd now caught the attention of two super-villains. And really, really bad ones at that.

I pulled my car into the hospital parking lot, in the area reserved for doctors. From experience I knew they didn't mind.

As I stepped out of the car, my skin prickled with awareness. I threw a glance over my shoulder. Just rows and rows of cars.

I turned my attention back to the hospital. What would it be this time—the burn unit, or the oncology department? Just as it usually did, excitement was replacing guilt. Whose lives would I change today?

As it happened, my footsteps led me to the neonatal intensive care unit, where several nurses swarmed in and out.

Today it would be a little bundle of joy. Thankfully, I didn't see any parents at the moment. I probably wouldn't make it back out without a broken plea or two, but for now I was okay.

I chose my patients based on their need, not on the persuasive power of parents, which meant that I made enemies even as I saved lives.

"Angel," a nurse breathed when she caught sight of me.

At the name, the others turned towards the doorway. "Angel!" another said. People had seen me on TV; they knew my face and recognized my gold jumpsuit.

"Are you here to ... help?" one asked.

I nodded. "Which of your patients is most in need?" I asked.

"Little Brandon over here," the nurse led me to him.

When it came to the premature babies, I'd noticed it was usually the boys that had the worst complications. Strange that for a gender that could become so fierce and strong, they were more vulnerable than their female counterparts at this age.

The nurse didn't tell me what was wrong with him— they never did.

I scrubbed up, needlessly following hospital policy, my pulse hiking. Today I'd save a life other than my own.

The nurses led me back to Brandon, and they removed a portion of his incubator so that I could reach inside.

I stared down at the tiny baby. He looked so delicate. Dropping my hand in, my finger smoothed down his soft cheek and reached for his tiny fist. I held it between my thumb and forefinger and waited.

When his face scrunched up and he began to cry, I removed my hand and stepped away.

Whatever little Brandon's medical issues were, now

they were gone.

By the time I pulled up to L.A.S.D.'s headquarters, a.k.a., Madcap Mansion—named so because we were all bat-shit crazy—it was almost ten at night. I could hear music blaring from one of the rooms, and shouts and laughter coming from another.

It was the Justice League meets Animal House—the Real World, superhero style. I lived here with over three dozen of L.A.S.D.'s finest.

"Duck!" came a scream from inside as I opened the door. I dropped to my knees just as a bolt of lightning sailed through the doorway above me. I slipped inside and sauntered over to the kitchen.

I grabbed a slice of pizza from the box in the kitchen and popped open a beer. I normally didn't drink, but after the day I had, alcohol was in order.

A moment later, Shadow materialized beside me. "Are you going to do Skinny-Dip Sunday with us this week?"

"Hells yeah," I said, heading out of the kitchen.

"Perfect." She winked out of existence.

Pizza in one hand and a Corona in the other, I made my way to the living room, the source of most of the shouts.

"*...two outs, bases are loaded.*"

Oh baby Christmas elves, The Game was on. I sprinted the rest of the way, vaulting over a recliner someone dragged into the hallway. I shoved a bite of pizza into my mouth as I stopped in front of the screen.

"Angel, get out of the way!" A peanut bounced off of

me.

Not looking away from the screen, I stepped aside. A little.

Bottom of the ninth. I'd practically missed the game. And my team was losing, two to three.

"Rodriguez is up to bat."

I held my breath as the pitcher threw one strike, then one ball. Then ...

Ohmygod, ohmygod, *ohmygod!* I screamed, my food forgotten, as Manny Rodriguez knocked the ball into the outfield.

Runners sprinted around the bases while the outfielders ran for the ball. As soon as the second man crossed the home plate, I spilled a little of my beer doing a victory dance.

Behind me I heard Rocket groan and Zephyr say, "Fork over the money, my man."

"Angels won, *again,*" I sing-songed.

A bitter Rocket muttered, "You only like them because you're their mascot."

"Awww," I made a pouty face at Rocket, "don't be a poor loser. I'm sure the Rockies will pull through next time."

"It's a 'poor sport' and a 'sore loser,' Angel."

"And you're both."

He flipped me off, which I sort of deserved. I smiled and took another bite of pizza, then waved it at the room. "Bye lovelies, I'm off."

I sauntered down the hall, ducking when another bolt of lightening almost singed me. What started out as a sucky day had come full circle. Regardless, I hoped tomorrow would be better.

Coming up to my room, I shoved the pizza in my mouth and, after wiping a greasy hand down my pantsuit, opened the door.

I flipped on my light and kicked the door shut. Closing my eyes, I breathed in a contented sigh. Home sweet home.

My skin prickled the same way it had earlier today. My eyes snapped back open. Leaning against the far wall was the Executioner.

He'd broken into my room. My mutha-fucking sanctuary.

My spine stiffened. The Executioner was inside Madcap Mansion. *The Executioner was inside Madcap Mansion.*

Shi-it. If I didn't want to set him loose on my friends, I needed to move my happy ass out of superhero headquarters ASAP.

"What are you doing here?" I breathed.

He stood there, his body blending with the shadows, and watched me. "I think you already know."

"You seriously thought you could snatch me from my own room?"

He didn't respond. No, the douchelord simply closed the distance between us and plunged a syringe into my neck.

CHAPTER 5

I REACHED OUT and ran my hand down Angel's face. I could touch her. Would my wonder ever diminish?

Her head leaned against the passenger side window of my car. I'd had to inject a sedative into her bloodstream to keep her out until I got her to my place. A *strong* one, otherwise her body would've worked it out of her system too soon.

Still, it wouldn't last long.

I slowed the car at a stoplight, then glanced over at the superhero beside me. Now that her sharp eyes no longer focused on me, I could study her. Caramel colored hair, skin that held just a touch of tan, sweet, soft lips.

With the pad of my finger I traced those lips—lips I'd

kissed. How had I never realized before that her abilities would cancel my own?

I scowled. What if I'd been mistaken? What if what happened earlier was a fluke?

I drew my hand away. No, not possible. Panic lanced through my veins. After all this time, I'd finally gotten a taste of what I'd been missing, and now I needed more. The thought of that single encounter being it ... the idea was too terrifying to comprehend.

I pulled off to the side of the road. *Have to check.*

Leaning across the console, I studied her cheek and lips. Unblemished. The others I'd touched always had blisters or red, swollen skin, no matter how careful I was.

Still. Perhaps the damage was internal.

I placed my ear next to Angel's heart, ignoring the swell of her breasts. The organ thumped away. Good enough for now. I'd wake her once we arrived at my Malibu home.

And to think that I dreaded coming to L.A. for this capture. Perhaps she'd exorcise some of my horrific childhood memories of this place.

There it was again—hope.

Don't get ahead of yourself, X. She will hate you at first.

I stared at her for a long moment before steering the car back to the road.

I'd work on extinguishing her hatred later. Right now, I needed to get her back to my place before she woke and tried to escape. Only then would she be mine to do with as I wished.

And how I'd wished.

MADMAN WAS BUSY losing to Aries in *Halo* when the vision hit him. He dropped his controller and clutched the sides of his head.

"Dude, no fakeouts just because you're getting owned," Aries said, his eyes pinned to the TV.

"Not ... faking it." Madman was no longer inside his namesake, Madcap Mansion. Instead he found himself in a dark bedroom. At its center rested a bed, and on it was Angel.

"Angel ..." he whispered.

"What about Angel, Madman?" The voice echoed from some distant place. Was he here or there? Could never tell.

"Where have you taken me?" Angel asked.

"I don't know," Madman said aloud. "You tell me."

"Huh?" Aries said.

"You are in your new home," a deep voice said.

Madman's gaze strayed from Angel. In a shadowy corner of the room, a man watched her, arms folded. The black jacket he wore fit like a second skin, and a hood covered all but his nose and lips.

The Executioner.

"*No, not Angel,*" Madman choked out.

"What's happening to Angel? What are you seeing?" that distant voice asked.

Madman couldn't answer, not when his attention was focused wholly on Angel. She was his favorite, though he'd never admit it. Pure of heart, contagious laughter. She'd pulled him from the edge of madness over and over again.

And now she was going to die.

Angel

I WOKE ON a bed. Don't remember falling asleep.

I blinked away my grogginess, and my surroundings came into focus. When I took in the dark walls, the shaded windows, and strange furniture, my brows knit together.

I pushed myself up so that my back rested against the bed's headboard, and I rubbed my eyes, stifling a yawn. My hands were left unbound.

Across the room a floorboard creaked, and my attention snapped to it. Against the darkened wall stood a deeper shadow. A human-shaped shadow.

The Executioner.

The last moments of lucidity came back to me. I must've been drugged and abducted. From my room in Madcap Mansion. We'd never had a security breach before. Not until tonight.

I scoured the room again. "Where am I?" I asked. Fear never factored into the equation. I was the hunter, not the hunted.

The Executioner stepped out of the shadows. "You are in your new home."

"My new home?" I raised an eyebrow. He thought he could just keep me here like some kind of sex slave? I smiled at that amusing thought. "I don't think so, amigo."

"Oh, but I do." The Executioner stepped to the foot of the bed and lifted his hood. All dark features and dangerous planes. He had the kind of violent beauty that killed you as you drew it in. Literally.

I rubbed my sternum. "Have you ... touched me?"

The Executioner's mouth curved into a sinful smile.

He had.

"Where?"

His hand dropped to his jacket's zipper, and he began removing the fitted material. The Executioner was undressing himself at the foot of the bed I was on. "All you need to know, Angel, is that I saved the best for last."

CHAPTER 6

Angel

"YOU'RE CRAZY IF you think I'm staying here," I said.

The bastard smirked, shrugging off his jacket. "Then leave," he said, stepping aside.

I stared at him as I maneuvered myself off his bed. His eyes tracked every one of my movements. "Why would you bring me here if you were planning on letting me go?"

He stayed silent for a long time. "I don't," he finally said.

"Are you going to try to kill me again?" I asked, eyeing the door next to him.

"Not now that I can touch you." He wanted to make the switch from killer to lover. Pretty ambitious move. Naturally, my wants weren't factored in.

"And you think I'm going to let you touch me again?" I asked.

"I know it," his voice dropped low, almost a growl. The way he said that sent shivers down my spine.

"I want to leave."

The Executioner gestured to the door. "Then go ahead and try."

I arched an eyebrow. "Try? You think I can't walk right out of here?"

A confident smile spread across his face, though it never reached his dark eyes. In them I could see anger and hunger simmering just beneath the surface.

What a disturbed, lonely creature. I was so used to laying my hands on people and healing them that I took a step towards him before I remembered myself.

Don't give him exactly what he wants, Angel. My attention moved to the open door and the hallway beyond.

This must be some sort of trap, I thought as I cautiously left the room and entered the corridor. *Some way for me to play directly into the man's hand.*

The Executioner followed me out. I walked down the hall and glanced out a nearby window. I was on the second story of what appeared to be a large estate in the hills. Of Los Angeles? Or somewhere else? And even if we were still in LA, were we in the Hollywood hills, Malibu, or Palace Verdes? Nothing about the view immediately gave our location away.

I headed for the staircase at the end of the hall and took the stairs down. The den I found myself in was windowless. I walked through it and into the next room. Another windowless space. As I passed into the next room, I found myself back in the den at the foot of the staircase I'd just descended.

Huh? I could've sworn I hadn't circled back.

The Executioner walked up next to me. I absently noticed he'd fisted his hands. *To keep from touching me?*

I scowled at him "Your floor plans make no sense."

He shrugged, heading past me to a bar nestled into a nearby alcove, where he grabbed a bottle of whiskey and began pouring himself a drink.

I let out a huff of irritation and climbed up the original staircase, only to find myself on a new floor. Walking over to a window, I peered outside again.

Damn it. It looked like I was on the third floor, but I could've sworn I returned back to the second floor. I rubbed my temples. I was turning into Madman, minus the soothsaying abilities.

At least from this view I could see glittering blue water in the distance. That removed the Hollywood hills.

I wandered around this floor until I hit another staircase that appeared to descend back down. What the hell, I might as well check it out. I walked down what felt like an eternity of stairs only to arrive in an entryway. And patiently waiting for me on the other end of the entryway was a large, carved door.

Success! Or, as Latin soccer announcers put it, *goooooaaaaal.*

I stalked towards it. Grabbing the handle, I yanked the door open. And came face to face with a brick wall.

I TOOK A sip of whiskey, silently thanking Mirage, the master of illusions, for her work on my place. She happened to be a good friend—perhaps *comrade* was a better term. There were no friends in my line of work, just individuals banded together by similar needs.

In exchange for the death of one of her longstanding enemies, she'd pimped out my home with illusions to confuse the hell out of visitors. Because the only visitors I ever had were unwelcome ones.

At least, until now.

Now the mirages would help keep Angel in. My Angel. Yeah, I was getting used to being proprietary as fuck when it came to her.

I tipped back the glass of whiskey.

"What the hell?"

My lips curled up at the corners at the sound of her voice. She was learning that escape was impossible unless I willed it.

And I did not will it.

I could hear her stomping around on the floor above me. I swallowed down the last of the whiskey and, setting the empty glass on a nearby table, I took the stairs to the first floor just in time to hear a crash.

Fuck.

I found her in the living room. She'd already managed to rip my flatscreen from the wall. It lay in pieces on the floor.

She breathed heavily, and in her hand she held a Minoan stirrup jar I'd stolen from the Athens Museum a few years ago. A priceless piece. I had sticky fingers when it came to valuable objects.

As soon as Angel caught sight of me, she cocked her arm back and hurled the vase at me. I caught it with a grunt. Girl had an arm on her.

"What do you think you're doing, woman?" I said, my anger flaring. I set the piece of pottery on a nearby table.

"Get me the hell out of here, or I'm going to destroy your entire place."

My jaw tightened. "Are you threatening *me?*"

In response, Angel walked over to a bookcase that showcased souvenirs from my travels, her wavy hair bouncing with her gait. *So goddamn lovely.*

She didn't even hesitate when she reached it. She simply grabbed the wood siding and yanked the bookcase forward.

"*No.*" I was moving, but it was too late.

The bookshelf tipped forward, my heavier souvenirs sliding off first and then the rest following.

The sound of the crash was all I needed—to—snap.

Angel

I TURNED, MY eyes prowling the room for the next object to destroy. Before they landed on anything, I caught sight of the Executioner.

His cheeks were sucked in with anger. Then they expanded out as he exhaled, then back in again. His nostrils flared. Pissed off didn't begin to describe the rage on his face.

He stalked towards me, his movements fluid.

Right about now the captain's earlier words echoed in my head. *Get the hell out of there.*

Working on it, captain.

I spun on my heel and fled in the opposite direction, down a darkened hallway. At the end of it, a staircase waited. Had I already climbed this one? Did it matter at the moment?

I dashed up it and found myself on the third floor. Unlikely that the exit out would be here, but who knew? This place had no logic to it.

I rounded the hall only to halt in my tracks. There the Executioner waited for me.

CHAPTER 7

Angel

THE EXECUTIONER STRODE towards me, his face eerily calm now.

"H-how did you beat me here?" I asked.

He ignored my question and continued to prowl forward, forcing me to back up until I bumped into the wall behind me. Still he kept coming.

When he reached me, his arms came up, pinning me in. He leaned in close. "You are not to destroy my things," he warned, his voice low.

"Then let me go."

"*Never*," he said with frightening vehemence. "Never, Angel."

At least I knew where he stood on this. I'd have to hunker down and wait for him to take his eyes off of me for a hot five seconds, and then I was *outta* here.

We stared at each other. The longer we stayed in this position, the more that rage of his dissipated. Eventually, it died away completely, morphing into something just as tense but much more ... titillating.

The Executioner broke eye contact first, his gaze pulled to my mouth. The want in his eyes ... I swore he fought the urge to lean forward and kiss me.

Instead his focus moved down to the hollow of my throat. Almost tentatively he brought his hand up and touched the skin there.

I closed my eyes and drew in a ragged breath. *No pain. None at all.* Actually, his touch felt quite pleasant.

Supervillain, Angel.

I froze when I felt him press his cheek against my breast. The position was strangely intimate, despite the layers of material that separated us.

"You heart hasn't even slowed," he said, his voice breathless. *With excitement,* I realized. The Executioner was excited that he hadn't hurt me.

I'd never even considered the possibility that the Executioner might not want to torture and kill. He did it so often that I assumed he enjoyed it.

Without thinking, I ran a hand through the Executioner's hair.

He made a soft noise in his throat, as though the sensation was pure ecstasy. When was the last time he'd touched or been touched by another without pain involved? Ever?

My hand curled in his hair, and I breathed in and

out through my nose. I was a healer, a fixer, and pressed against me was the most broken, screwed up person I'd ever met. Dang it all, I did not want to feel affection for the man that tried to kill me, the same person who now held me hostage.

I let my hand drop and pushed him away from me. "This isn't happening, Executioner. I'd rather die than be with a villain like you."

Executioner

AFTER HEARING THAT damn heartbeat of hers against my ear, I thought I must be dreaming. And when I felt her hand slide through my hair *affectionately*, I knew I was delusional.

Because something this good never happened to a monster like me.

So when Angel spoke, her words slapped me back into the present.

I straightened. "I'm not asking."

She was mine. That was the end of it. Even if every other healer in the world had her same penchant for neutralizing my ability, I doubted I'd be interested. Already the green of her eyes had become my favorite color, and her slight build my favorite body type. Even now I was imagining the rest of what lay beneath her clothes. What it would feel like to lay flush with her and not have to worry about burning her delicate skin.

What it would be like to slide into her sweet folds and lay claim to her.

I scooped Angel up and began walking down the hall.

"What are you doing?" No fear in her voice. Alarm and annoyance, maybe, but not fear.

Good.

I wound my way back to my bedroom. Here she'd be protected, and here she couldn't escape.

Behind me the door clicked shut.

"Now the two of us are going to get to know each other," I said.

She laughed, the sound pleasing.

Need to make her laugh more often.

"Oh we are now?" she said, her tone taunting. She relaxed a bit more into my arms. "What exactly did you have in mind?"

My cell vibrated in my pocket, and I almost groaned. Work at a time like this?

I dumped Angel onto the bed and reached for my phone.

"*Oomph!*" she grunted as she hit the mattress.

"I'm busy," I said, answering the call.

"God, you are such an A-hole!" Angel scrambled from the bed to her feet. "Like a huge one."

"Make time for me," said the Cruel Countess, a sinister bitch I couldn't trust farther than I could throw her. At least she paid well.

"What is it?" I asked.

"A competitor of mine received a shipment of goods and thought to cut me out of the arrangement," the Cruel

Countess said. "I need you to rectify the situation."

Eliminate the target. Simple enough.

"Which competitor?" Out of the corner of my eye, I saw Angel grab the door handle. It didn't budge.

I folded my arms and leaned back against the wall, settling in to watch her as I talked.

"Wrath." Who conveniently lived in L.A.

The Cruel Countess hadn't warned me about another assignment here, but I wasn't surprised. She liked to stack her business together when she could. I think she found it satisfying to wipe out several problems as efficiently as possible. And I was very efficient.

"When should I strike?"

"Today. Now preferably."

Of course right now.

I ran a hand under my chin. "It's as good as done."

Angel let out a frustrated shriek. "Damn you! Let me *out!*"

"Who is *that?*" Curiosity tinged the Cruel Countess's voice.

"A hooker."

"Ugh, pretend I didn't ask," the Cruel Countess said. "Anyway, make sure to send Wrath the message that I am not to be crossed."

My lips tightened into a hard line. "Fine."

Swiveling from the door, Angel stalked towards me. Oh this I liked.

"And Executioner?" the Cruel Countess said.

"Hmm?" I said, eyeing my woman. She had murder in her eyes, and I was growing hard at the sight.

"Any updates on the healer yet?"

"She was a no-show yesterday," I said, even as I stared down the superhero in question. "Mirage can vouch for me." Mirage couldn't, in fact, vouch for me because she scrammed as soon as she'd set up the illusion. *Have to call her later and fill her in.*

Angel closed the distance between us, practically spitting fire. All the rumors about her being sweet as a lamb were wrong.

"I want her, Executioner. Do it tomorrow." The line went dead.

Before I could pocket the phone, Angel jerked it from my grasp and threw it on the floor.

"What the—?"

The heel of her boot came down on the phone. Just when I thought she'd shatter the screen, her foot paused "Let me out, Executioner."

I narrowed my eyes. "Go ahead, Angel," I said, nodding to the device. "Break it."

She smiled. "Reverse psychology doesn't work on me."

Now it was my turn to grin. Menacingly. "I can get another phone. I can't get another you."

I turned away from her and strode towards the door, snatching my jacket from the floor and shrugging it on.

"Where are you going?"

Said like she expected me to stick around. This was a day of firsts.

I could get used to this.

I lifted my hood over my head. "I have business to attend. Think twice before ruining any more of my things."

I grabbed the knob and opened the door.

Angel's eyes darted to the action. "How did you open ...? Wait, no—!" Her voice cut out as the door shut behind me.

My Angel wasn't going anywhere anytime soon.

CHAPTER 8

Angel

I SCREAMED AS I kicked at the windows for the millionth time. And for the millionth time, they didn't budge from the impact—didn't even shudder. *Just like the solid oak door.*

I'd been stuck in this stupid room for hours. Ever since that prick put me in here.

I fell back on the Executioner's bed and stared up at the ceiling. I just *had* to act like a true prisoner. Perhaps if I'd tried to deceive him I'd have gotten better results.

Having these hours to myself did, however, give me plenty of time to think about my situation. The Executioner, for instance, might be completely evil, but he'd already revealed his weakness—touch. He craved it like a drowning man craved air.

He wouldn't kill me. He might not even hurt me—there had been several instances where I could've sworn he didn't want this violent life. But he wanted to touch me, and he was roguish enough to do whatever he thought necessary to reach that end goal. Like lock me in a room. Asshat.

After surviving my initial encounter with him, I also knew that he was singling out superheroes for some purpose. A steady stream of them had disappeared over the last two years, and I'd bet money that they'd received the same ultimatum I had. But why? What was the Executioner up to? Or, better yet, what was his boss, the Cruel Countess, up to?

I pinched my lower lip. If I could find out, then perhaps I could stem the tide of deaths. Could I earn the Executioner's trust? That might give me the opportunity to learn his plans and escape this place. Maybe even save some lives.

I turned my head into the Executioner's pillow and breathed in the smell of body wash and man. His scent. I scowled when I realized I liked it. And therein lay the one crucial problem with my plan: gaining his trust without accidently feeling more for him.

Executioner

I PULLED OFF my gloves as I drove back along the Highway 1. The last eight hours had been tedious, and my mind hadn't been fully in my work. Instead I kept drifting back to the woman in my bedroom.

I hadn't meant to stay away this long. Traffic and Wrath's penchant for preparing for the worst had lengthened the job. I should've left food in the room for Angel. I frowned. She'd gone hungry the entire day.

I pulled out my spare cell, my mouth tipping up at Angel's earlier antics. As though I didn't change phones frequently, given my line of business.

I dialed the Cruel Countess's number, my finger pausing over *Send.*

I'd never asked for this job as her enforcer. Coercion had been involved. No one knew that particular detail, though some of my comrades had to suspect. Just as I suspected that the Cruel Countess had ferreted out their weaknesses and used what she found against them.

Forced cooperation.

Shackled and gagged. My captors in hazmat suits. Her ultimatum ...

I shoved the memory away, swallowed my rage.

Even now that knife dangled over my neck. Once she learned I defied her, she'd take action. Angel's life wasn't the only one in danger now. I needed to make arrangements, buy myself time to form a plan.

But for now, I needed to handle the current situation.

I hit *Send* and pressed the phone to my ear.

"Is it done?" she answered.

"I expect five million wired to my account by the end of the day," I said by way of answer.

She sighed. "Your rates try my patience."

"Wrath's men will be coming down on my head in the near future. Consider it hazard pay."

"Fine, fine. And the girl?"

I felt my pulse hike at the mention of her. Excitement at the prospect of returning to her. Fear for the situation I'd now mired her in. "I kill people for a living," I said. "I don't stop time."

"Don't keep me waiting." The line went dead.

I tossed the phone onto the passenger seat and started the engine.

I couldn't put the Cruel Countess off forever. I'd need to come up with something soon.

If my enemies now knew I had another weakness ...

Only one more reason why I needed to keep Angel locked up. My foot pressed down on the gas. After the world's longest assignment, I'd finally get to see her.

I rubbed a hand over my jaw at the thought of Angel in my room. On my bed.

Don't get ahead of yourself.

She wasn't going to just give herself to me. Frustrating, intriguing woman. I would have to give chase and wear her down. That was what I was good at, wearing people down. That was all that torture was, after all, applied pressure over stretches of time.

I couldn't hold her against her will forever. She'd have to want to stay eventually. Problem was, I'd never done relationships. Not ones based on something other than money and mutually vested interest. Not ones based on love and sex.

And the thought of having sex with Angel ... I groaned

and adjusted myself. Fuck. I was no better than a horny teenager.

I needed to come up with a plan and then lay low for a while. Then I could get my personal affairs in order.

Personal affairs.

Shiit.

Angel

I JOLTED OUT of sleep, not sure what had woken me. I rubbed my eyes and sat up in the Executioner's bed. I squinted at the room's windows. Deep blue sky filtered in. Which meant I'd been here all evening.

A door slammed in the distance.

He's back.

Back from a day of marauding and killing—just the usual for a supervillain like himself.

Suddenly I was wide awake.

The Executioner's heavy footfalls got louder as he strode towards the room, now sounding up the stairs, now walking down the hall. My heart began to pound like it did before a raid. It was some strange mixture of anxiety and anticipation.

His steps halted in front of my room, and my breath caught. Every instinct inside me was telling me to ambush him and make a run for it. I had to fist my hands to keep from acting on the urge.

Win him over, learn his secrets, then escape, I chanted this to myself as the knob turned.

And there he stood in the doorway, his body filling the space out. He still wore his hood, and his characteristic black attire covered the rest of his body.

"Hello, Executioner," I said, lounging back against his bed. I wore one of his shirts and nothing else. He'd been *so kind* to leave the change of clothes for me in case I wanted to sleep.

Fucker.

Using both his hands, he removed the hood from his face. Underneath it, his eyes flickered hungrily over my body and his jaw clenched tightly. Flecks of blood dotted his face.

Yep, he'd been busy getting down and evil.

His eyes lingered on my sculpted legs before traveling upwards. Something possessive entered his features when he saw my breasts molded beneath his shirt. I smirked as his hands clenched and unclenched at his sides. Finally, his gaze moved to my face.

He exhaled. "Hello, Angel." He made my name sound like an endearment. He kicked the door closed, and I heard it click ominously.

Don't stare at it. Don't stare at it.

Anger simmered just below the surface of my skin. How dare this man think he could keep me, a superhero, here as his prisoner.

He brooded as he moved about his room. I got the impression, now that he had me, he didn't know what to do with me.

Time to start winning him over.

I pushed myself off of his bed and headed towards him. He eyed me warily as he tossed his gloves onto the top of his dresser.

Stopping in front of him, I gripped the zipper of his jacket. I think this was what he wanted—my interest and my touch. I'd give him both—to a limited extent.

I pulled the zipper down, the sound abnormally loud, especially now that the Executioner's breathing had gone quiet.

He watched me, mesmerized by my movements. The Executioner might never have experienced this casual seduction between a man and a woman. Even I, a twenty-three year old who was allergic to relationships, knew more about this than he did, and he looked to be several years older than me.

I snuck a glance down at his hands. Fisted. Meaning he was restraining himself a great deal. I was quickly learning all of his tells.

"What are you doing?" he asked, his voice rough.

I looked up at him. His jaw was tight with tension and his eyes glinted. Some long and drawn out war was going on behind that face of his.

"Removing your clothing," I said. The smile I gave him was sly.

As soon as I unzipped his jacket, I slid my hands beneath it and over his chest. Mmm, Torture Boy had a nice set of pecs. My touch moved up to his shoulders. Thick, corded muscle covered these too.

"Why would you do that?" he murmured.

I forced his jacket down his arms. Underneath it, he

wore a fitted T-shirt.

"Remove your clothing?" I asked, my gaze moving from his chest back to his face, where his eyes devoured me. "Because I want to. And because you have me here for this very reason. Or would you rather we play checkers and sing songs together? We can do that if you'd prefer." The Executioner's jacket hit the floor a second later, the sound punctuating my words.

"I can remove my own clothing," he growled.

"But then you can't chance one of my hands grazing your skin." As I spoke, I deliberately slid the tips of my fingers down his forearms.

His eyes darkened with want. All from my words. Toying with this supervillain was kind of fun. Much better than my usual experience with them, which usually involved lots of blood and pain.

I grabbed the edges of the black shirt he wore and yanked up, uncovering miles and miles of delicious muscles.

Le sigh. Bad guys always had the hottest bodies.

The Executioner helped me remove the shirt since he was considerably taller than me. And then he stood there, all his sculpted muscles on display. And no one to give this exquisite form love. I wanted to cry out on behalf of woman everywhere that no one had gotten to revel in these muscles before me.

I reached out to touch him, curious to see what reaction this would elicit.

The Executioner caught my wrist and almost dropped it before he remembered that I couldn't be killed by his touch. "Too fast," he said, closing his eyes.

"But you got to kiss me."

He nodded, his nostrils flaring. His eyes were still closed. "That was too fast."

Changing his tune now, was he?

The Executioner threaded his fingers through my own. "Goddamn," he murmured, opening his eyes to stare at our entwined hands.

He was soaking up my touch, savoring it like it was something decadent. And so help me, I was charmed to my toes.

He's a bad guy, Angel, not a neglected puppy.

But even as I thought it, a small voice whispered in my ear, *Maybe he's both.*

CHAPTER 9

Executioner

Under the hot spray of the shower, I leaned my head against the wall, an arm covering my eyes. I slammed the side of my fist against the tile, cracking it.

I'd practically fled my own room after Angel tried to finish undressing me. Fled, like one of my victims. And why? Because I was getting exactly what I wanted, and I couldn't fucking handle it. I was a masochist.

Not only that, but she'd been ready to steer me. Like that little thing knew more about seduction than I did.

Fuck, she probably did.

I slammed my hand into the tile again. Shards of glazed porcelain broke loose beneath my hand.

"Everything okay?" Angel's muffled voice called from

the other side of the door.

No. I'm coming apart for the first time in my life, and it's your damn fault.

Instead, I glanced at my now bleeding hand. A piece of the tile must've nicked me.

The door clicked open, and I cursed. "I didn't say you could enter."

"And I didn't ask," came her tart reply.

"Get out," I growled.

"Are you ... modest?"

In response, I opened the shower door and leaned my body against it. "Does it look like I'm modest?"

Her eyes widened at the sight of me, and she cleared her throat. "Nope."

"Get out of here."

Her chin lifted, the expression surly. "If you wanted to keep me out, you should've locked the door."

I ground my teeth together. It wasn't a good time for her to be in my space, not when I was this confused and frustrated. Usually when I felt this way, I throttled the idiot who pissed me off.

Can't do that to her—wouldn't want to.

For her, I'd have to be a little more original.

I pushed away from the shower, letting water drip down my body and onto the floor as I approached her. Angel's eyes skittered over me, and an unwilling smile drew the edges of her lips up. Until she caught a glimpse of my face.

Her smile slipped, and something like caution entered her features. Even as I tried to intimidate her, I didn't want to see that expression on her face. I didn't want her to be skittish around me.

So then, what did I want?

I backed her against the wall, crowding her for the second time since I'd taken her. "I am not someone to piss off," I warned.

She smiled at that like I was cute, not intimidated at all by the threat or the lack of space.

"You can get back in the shower, Executioner," she said. "I just want someone to talk to. You left me alone in your room all day."

I had. "You can't make me feel guilty about that," I said, reluctantly stepping back in the shower. I didn't know when I'd decided that she could stay in the room with me.

"Yeah, well, if you want to be my sugar daddy," she said, "you're going to have to get me clothes, books, my own personal TV—"

"So you can break it just like the last one?" I asked incredulously.

"If I wish to, yes. And I want it to have HBO, because that channel's got all the good shows. And I want movies, and make-up, and shoes, and bags, and—"

"Woman, you are giving me a headache," I said.

"My name is not 'woman.'"

I rubbed my forehead. How did one deal with these creatures? "I will get you amenities."

No wonder most men seemed fairly docile; their women had all browbeaten them into submission.

She made an approving sound.

"Eventually," I added.

"Eventually my ass."

I cracked my neck. "Last I noticed, you are the captive here."

She yanked open the shower door. "Yeah, and if you want me to be anything other than just your captive," she said, glancing downwards at my cock, "you'll pick these things up for me A-S-A-P."

Game. Set. Match.

Angel

THE EXECUTIONER HELD his towel around his waist as he walked out of the shower.

"Well, are you going to make me breakfast, Romeo?" I asked him.

While he was off murdering people, I'd had to drink water from the bathroom sink. The bathroom sink! Not to mention the lack of food. My superpower burned through calories like it was nobody's business, and I'd eaten nothing since he'd taken me. As far as gilded cages go, this one sucked balls.

The Executioner frowned at me, and I tried to ignore the way his damp hair curled around his temples. Giving his back to me, he dropped his towel.

I was unashamed to admit that I freely stared at his sculpted backside, and for one weak moment, I wondered what it would be like to be with a man like the Executioner.

While I wasn't a fan of relationships, no one would call me sexually repressed. I served the good people of LA in more ways than one.

Boom. And you get an orgasm.

"Will you just give me a moment?" he growled.

"Give you a moment?" I said incredulously, heading over to him. "You had hundreds of them while you left me stranded here." My stomach was cramping in on itself. "I want to eat. Now."

The Executioner reached into his closet, pulling out a set of clothes, then slammed the door. Oh, and he ignored me completely.

"Aggravating woman," the Executioner grumbled as he began slipping on his pants.

"'Aggravating'?" I repeated, blinking at his form. "You think I'm *aggravating*?" My voice had gone shrill.

He grunted in response.

Maybe it was a sugar low or simply the hypocrisy of it all. Whatever it was, I was done playing nice. I stalked towards him, my fingers curling and uncurling.

The bastard was going down.

CHAPTER 10

Executioner

I HAD JUST slipped on my pants when Angel jumped onto my back like a spider monkey. I didn't immediately react. After all, no one had ever attacked me like this. No one was that crazy. Or stupid.

Except for this broad.

Her forearm wrapped around my neck. "I will make you pay for that, Executioner." She squeezed my neck with her arm, cutting off my blood circulation.

The little thing was trying to use a sleeper hold on me.

I grabbed her wrist to pry her off, but already my vision clouded. Damn, she was good at it too.

"You—are—a—psycho," I wheezed.

And then the room went dark.

Angel

As soon as the Executioner's legs folded under him, I jumped off his back and stared down at him.

You just pissed off the wrong girl, amigo.

I kicked him in the happy sacs, just to punctuate the thought.

When he groaned, I planted another swift kick to his head. I needed to make sure he was comatose while I gave as good as I got.

First I changed back into my suit, then I checked the door. Locked, again. I glanced back at my captor.

Crouching next to him, I hooked my arms under the Executioner's and began to drag him towards the door. I hadn't been able to leave this room, but he had.

Time to test a theory. That was, if I could manage to move him into place.

"You ... weigh more ... than my grandma," I grunted as I lugged him across the room. "And she was ... no dainty thing."

What was this guy made of? Lead?

When I reached the door, I wrapped one of the Executioner's hands around the handle and turned it. The door swung open. Hallelujah! I dropped his arm and used his body as a doorjamb until I replaced it with a book from his nightstand.

I threaded my fingers over my head. One problem down. Now to drag this ho's butt to the bed.

My biceps spasmed at the thought. I was so buying myself a chocolate banana milkshake from Swifty's Dairy Delights once these shenanigans were over. And a corndog. Or a Slurpee. I deserved at least that for surviving this mess of a man.

Using all my straining muscles, I lugged the Executioner back across the room. I hefted him face-first onto his bed, and then, pushing his ass, nudged the rest of his body onto the mattress.

... I might've also copped a feel in the process. All I will say is, *damn son.* The guy had an excellent backside on him.

Fucking villains. They always had to be the sexy, single ones.

Once the Executioner was on his bed, I flipped his body over, my eyes lingering on his face. His dark lashes kissed the tops of his cheeks, and his mouth lost its cruel tilt. Unconscious, the Executioner was perhaps even more gorgeous than he was awake.

Or maybe it's because he can't open his big ol' mouth and tell you that you're aggravating or psychotic.

I made my way to his closet. From my earlier exploration I'd found his belt stash, and I'd plotted for exactly this situation. Though, to be honest, a tiny part of me was kind of hoping I'd get a little action before then.

A girl only gets propositioned by a supervillain so many times in her life.

I grabbed his entire collection of leather belts and made my way back to the bed.

We'd see just how much the Executioner liked me after this.

Executioner

WHEN I CAME to, Angel was straddling my torso.

Too good to be real life. Must be a dream.

I heard Angel grunt and my shoulders yanked up. "You're awake," she said. "Just in time too."

Not a dream, after all.

I squinted, my head beginning to pound. I tried to sit up just as she swung a leg off of me and found that I couldn't move.

What in the hell?

I jerked my hands only to feel them resist my pull. I glanced up and noticed they'd been bound together above my head.

Angel let out another soft grunt, and my leg jerked. I looked back down my body and saw her tightening a leather belt that pinned my ankle to the corner of the bed.

"I am not the type of girl that gives out pity fucks," she said, conversationally. "Sorry."

"*What is the meaning of this?*" I shouted, kicking out and trying to sabotage her efforts.

She buckled the restraints in place. "Aww, is someone a little upset?" She pouted her lips.

I roared. "Unhand me, woman!"

And then she laughed in my face. "You self-satisfied, prideful prick. I'll do no such thing." She crept forward and knelt beside the bed. Propping her elbow on the mattress, she leaned her chin in her hand. "Tell me, how does it feel to be the imprisoned one?"

Anger pulsed through my veins. The last time I'd felt this helpless, I'd gone on a rampage. Did she not realize who she was dealing with?

Every vessel in my body strained against the bindings. I could hear the leather groan and the wooden frame begin to splinter as it gave under my force.

Angel stood and backed up, undaunted by the sound. She held up my keys, and I paused in my efforts. She must've plucked them right out of my pocket. "I'll be going now," she said.

My eyes flicked from the keys to her face. It was my turn to laugh. "You can't get out of here," I said arrogantly. "Not without me." That was how Mirage's illusions worked.

She leaned forward. "You forgot one thing."

I raised my eyebrows. "Oh, did I?"

Angel smiled. "I'm a fucking superhero. Bitch."

CHAPTER 11

Angel

WHAT TO DO, *what to do.*

I stalked back and forth across the Executioner's living room. Since I'd delivered that exit line, dropped the metaphorical mike, and left the supervillain trapped in his own room, I hadn't been able to figure out just how to leave this ridiculous mansion.

Nope. All I'd done was nurse a couple of nearly dead plants in the kitchen back to life. Oh, and close my eyes and savor the sound of the Executioner bellowing. Better than chocolate—and *that* was saying something.

But the longer I stalled, the more likely he was to break his bindings and hunt me down. I shivered. I didn't want to be here when that happened.

I glanced at the front door again. I knew enough about villains to know this was the work of Mirage. As was the burning building the Executioner had baited me with.

The issue was, Mirage's illusions were masterpieces. They were interactive and lifelike. But they couldn't alter reality; they could only trick the mind.

I glanced at the car key in my hand. It was one of those smart car keys. The supervillain had a nice ride. Figures.

Problem—for him—was that you could lock and unlock a vehicle with one of these things even if a wall separated you from your car. And, if you hit it often enough, the car would beep.

I began to wander the house while clicking the unlock button. I paused when I heard the chirp of a horn. I tilted my head and listened. The sound came from a shadowy room down the hall.

I entered it and repeated the process until I heard the car beep again. This time the sound came from the back of the room.

Stepping up to the nearest wall, I placed my hand against its surface and began to pace the room, dragging my hand along it as I went. I cursed when it banged into what felt like a bookcase, and again when I almost knocked down a lamp. Stupid mirages.

Eventually my fingers ran into a lip. Skimming both hands over the area I felt the edges of some kind of molding that the mirage covered up. The door!

I searched around until my hand bumped into the doorknob.

"Gotcha," I whispered.

I'd found my way out.

Executioner

I HAD ALMOST broken free of my bonds when I heard the roar of an engine. My car's engine.

Angel was escaping and hijacking *my* car.

If I was going to get out of these damn bindings I'd have to do it now. I strained my muscles, clenching my jaw as the leather groaned.

I shouted as the belts dug into my skin. She couldn't get away. Not when I'd just found her. Not when the Cruel Countess was hunting her down. The wood creaked and splintered under my force.

No retribution. I'd set aside my anger so long as I got her back. But I *would* get her back.

Just a bit more pressure.

My teeth scraped together and sweat beaded along my forehead. All at once the bed's wooden frame let out a screech, and then it collapsed in on itself.

Free.

Angel

I NERVOUSLY CHEWED on a thumbnail as I drove the Executioner's black Lotus down the windy Malibu hills, finally recognizing my surroundings. We hadn't left L.A., which meant I could get back to Madcap Mansion soon.

As for the Executioner, I'd left him tied up in his room, but now I had some real decisions to make.

He was too dangerous to be allowed to live. I slowed the car. I should go back and finish this—terminate a threat.

I pulled onto the shoulder of the road and put a hand to my forehead. Trying to detain him was pointless. History had already taught the world what would happen when you tried to incarcerate a bad guy too powerful to be stopped. The end result had always been the same: massive prison breaks and lots of casualties.

I'd need to kill him or convince him to change his ways.

I swallowed. I really didn't want to kill him, and I wasn't completely sure why. I'd taken out other bad guys in the line of duty, bad guys whose crimes paled in comparison to those of the Executioner.

Maybe he reminded me a little too much of those at-risk kids, only he'd never been saved. With a power like his, he'd probably been doomed from the very start. A victim who'd never been saved—never even gotten the chance.

I could be that chance. Was it too late to go back to him?

A car curved around the corner ahead of me, and I shielded my eyes as its headlights obscured my vision. I heard the purr of the car's V8 engine and the blasted lyrics of "Baby Got Back."

It slammed to a stop in front of me, and someone jumped out. I squinted. Wait ...

"*Aries?*" And now that I got a better look, was that vehicle the Red Rider?

Aries crossed over to my car and opened the door. "What the … ?"

"Sorry babe, but I'm only doing Madman's bidding."

I furrowed my brows. "Madman … ?"

Madman leaned out of the backseat of the car. "That's your cue, Aries."

My eyes widened with understanding just as Aries's fist slammed into my face.

CHAPTER 12

Angel

"'DA FUCK?" I asked, blinking as I came to.

Sir Mix-a-Lot was still playing from the stereo, the bass thumping and making my head pound. A man's arms wrapped around my waist, and my back rested against his torso.

I glanced up. Aries was watching me, his expression apologetic, as the car roared down the road.

"Why the hell did you punch me?"

He shrugged. "Madman told me to."

I felt a pat on my knee, and I glanced over. Madman smiled, his eyes far away.

"What's going on?" I tried to push away from Aries, but his hold only tightened.

"We're rescuing you," Zephyr said from the driver's seat. Next to her, Shadow's head bobbed to the music.

"Rescuing me?" My eyes widened in understanding. This was Madman's doing; he must've had a vision of my capture as well as my escape. "No—no, no, no, no. I need to get back."

"Angel, you can't fix the guy," Zephyr said, glancing at me through the rearview mirror.

How did she know that exact thought had run through my head only moments ago?

My eyes moved back to Madman. *Because he's seen that too.*

"You need to let me go," I said more insistently, struggling against Aries. He didn't loosen his grip.

After a few moments, I stopped fighting; I couldn't possibly overpower the guy with inhuman strength.

"Weeeeee!" Madman said. One side of his mouth curved up and his eyes were glazed over, lost in another one of his episodes.

"The Executioner's not going to do anything to me," I insisted to the rest of the car.

"How can you be so sure?" Aries said.

"He can't kill me."

Sir Mix-a-Lot's voice and the growl of an approaching car were the only sounds that punctuated the silence.

Finally, "Shiiit," Aries drawled. He glanced over at Madman accusingly. "You didn't tell us *that*."

Madman cackled.

"That's why you guys need to let me go," I said. "I'm the only one that can deal with him."

"Deal with him?" Zephyr said. "What does that mean? That you'll bang him to death? Cause, honey, we all know you aren't going to pop a cap in his ass."

I glared at the back of Zephyr's head. Behind us the sound of an engine rose, getting louder as it neared.

"Face it, Angel," Shadow said, "your strength is saving, not killing."

"What makes you think the Executioner can't be saved?" I asked.

"Some people are beyond saving," Aries said, his tone harsh.

Zephyr glanced at the rearview mirror. "Some asshole is riding our tail."

Madman put his hands in the air, and Zephyr's gaze flicked to him. "What are you—?"

I registered the roar of the tailgater's engine a split second before it rammed into ours. Metal crunched, Aries and I toppled over the center console.

Heavy dude on my back. Can't breathe.

"Aries," I wheezed, "get off ... of me."

Just as he began to, the car rammed us again, and Aries slid forward, crushing me further.

The car veered off the road and we began to bounce over the rough terrain. But we weren't slowing.

I looked up and caught sight of a guardrail, and beyond that ... nothing.

"Thing's lost traction," Zephyr said. "Fuck, we're going to go over!"

That was all the warning we got. With a sickening screech, the front of our car hit the guardrail. The metal barrier gave way, and then we were airborne.

As we flew through the air, Aries shrieked. *If we all survive, he's never living that down.* Behind us, Madman was laughing like this was the funniest thing in the world, and Sir Mix-a-Lot was still aggressively campaigning the perks of big booties.

We plummeted over the edge of the mountain. The earth seemed to rise up to meet us, and I braced myself for the next moment of impact. As soon as the car connected with the ground, Aries and I—who hadn't been wearing seatbelts—were flung through the car's front window.

I screamed as we broke through the windshield. Shards of glass sliced my skin, and then rocks replaced glass as we tumbled onto the ground. The car continued to roll down the hill, the metal crumpling in on itself and the rest of the team.

I crawled to Aries, blinking away blood from a head wound as my injuries healed themselves. Blood covered his face and body, and one of his arms was bent funny. I reached over and touched his face.

His eyes pinched shut and he gritted his teeth while his arm reset itself and his cuts began to seal. From somewhere on the street above us, our pursuer's engine cut out.

The Executioner. It had to be him.

"Your boyfriend ... is a dick," Aries gasped out, sweat beading along his brow.

Guess I wasn't the only person to put two and two together.

When I'd decided Aries's broken bone had fully fused back together, I let go of him and dusted myself off.

Above us a car door opened.

"Aries, I'm going to help the others. If the Executioner comes for me, don't try to stop him."

Aries groaned as he sat up. "Like hell I won't. That bastard just tried to kill us. He *will* kill us."

My eyes flicked up the mountain. I heard a car door slam shut. "He won't kill me," I murmured. And then I ran to the wreckage below.

Executioner

I SHOULD MURDER *them all just to prove she can never leave me.*

Even before I had come across my abandoned Lotus, I'd caught sight of the Red Rider, one of L.A.S.D.'s ridiculous cars, winding further down the mountain road. I'd easily put together what must've happened.

Angel's quaint little justice league had tried to pull off a rescue mission.

And now they all would pay for trying to cross me.

I exited the car and stepped up to the broken guardrail.

Superheroes were scattered like confetti down the mountainside. Closest to me was Aries, the muscle of the group. And right now he was squaring off with me, waiting for me to make the first move.

Because he can't kill me, but I can kill him.

Beyond Aries, Angel crouched next to the crumpled wreckage, reaching her hands inside the Red Rider. She kept throwing furtive glances over her shoulder. When she noticed me staring, she froze.

"You can't have her, Executioner."

My gaze flicked back to Aries. Killing him would set Angel and me back a bit, but after the day I'd had, I was tempted.

Aries stepped forward. "You're going to have to go through me to get to her."

I stepped over the remains of the guardrail, my clothes snapping in the night air. No one would keep me from Angel. Not my colleagues, not my enemies, and not this man in front of me.

I strode down the hill towards him. I'd seen footage of this superhero lifting cars like they were sacks of groceries. That inhuman strength wouldn't save him. Not from me.

I could see Angel starting to panic from where she crouched, her head moving between the two of us.

I began to work a glove off as I neared Aries. Today I'd already seen my fair share of blood, but there was always room for more.

Angel

I LOOKED UP from my arm, which Madman, Zephyr and Shadow held onto, back to Aries and the Executioner.

He was going to kill Aries. I could see it in the Executioner's eyes.

"Stop!" I screamed, my heart thundering in my chest.

The Executioner glanced up. He was only mere feet

from Aries.

"Time to let go of Angel," Madman said to the others in the car. They released my arm, and I pushed away from the car.

"The only way you're getting me out of here," I said to the Executioner, "is if you leave my friends untouched."

"You really think that, Angel?" His voice carried clearly on the night air. "I could take them all out—them and every other person that might stand between you and me."

What *was* to stop him? He was a gun for hire. He probably killed people even when he didn't mean to. Ridding Los Angeles of its superheroes would be nothing to him, and now I gave him an extra reason to do it.

I began to climb up the hill, towards both him and Aries, the latter who shifted his weight between his feet. I stumbled a little as I went. The Executioner noticed, and I saw him frown.

Behind me, I could hear the grunts and moans of the rest of my friends as they began to extricate themselves from the Red Rider.

Right now there was an uneasy standoff, but I couldn't delude myself: the balance of power was wholly tipped in the Executioner's favor.

"I will go back with you," I said to him. "I won't fight it. Just—don't touch any of my friends."

He gave me a look that sent shivers down my back. For the life of me I had no idea what was going on in his head, but I did know that despite his reputation, he wouldn't hurt me.

Aries snagged my arm as I approached the Executioner.

"Don't be an idiot," he hissed into my ear. "We don't give into villains' demands. Not now, not ever." He glanced at the Executioner as he spoke, but his words were lost on the man. The Executioner hadn't looked away from me since I'd spoken. And his hands.

Clench ... unclench.

"Today is the exception," I said, my skin prickling from how close Aries still was to that lethal touch.

"Angel," he pleaded softly.

I pulled my arm out of his grip. "Go get our friends and get out of here."

The Executioner stepped forward and held out a hand to me. His chin was tilted up; he commanded with his presence.

I stared at that hand. "Don't hurt my friends," I warned him.

He said nothing, but inclined his head ever so slightly.

I took a step forward. Then another.

Aries made a grab for my wrist. "Angel, *don't.*"

I shrugged off his arm. "I'll be fine. Help the others." My gaze never wavered from the Executioner's. "And don't come for me again."

Ahead of me, the Executioner gave me a grim smile. I reached out and grasped his bare hand. The moment I did so, his grip clamped down, as if he thought I might still run.

I heard Aries suck in air and somewhere down the hill, a couple gasps. And then, when I didn't start screaming, I heard my team's murmurs.

"*Fuck. He really can't hurt Angel.*"

"*What's he going to do to her?*"

"*What do you think genius?*"

I suppressed a cringe at that last line. The Executioner's grim smile grew a little bigger; I guess he'd heard the line as well.

"This changes things," he said to me.

"It changes *nothing.*"

His eyes narrowed. "Just remember that you came willingly."

CHAPTER 13

Angel

THE EXECUTIONER RUBBED his raw wrists as he drove us back to his suburban fortress. The drive was quiet. Tense.

"You are going to sleep in my bed, tonight."

"True, I am going to sleep in your bed tonight. But you aren't going to be in it."

His hands squeezed the steering wheel. "You are to listen to me—"

"Gah, your people skills suck balls. *I'm not sleeping with you*, nor am I sleeping in the same room as you because—in case you forgot—you just tried to *kill* my friends after *imprisoning* me in a goddamn room for an *entire day*."

This was what I got for helping others. A psycho supervillain who badly wanted to get laid.

The Executioner's jaw tightened. "We will discuss this when we get home."

His words rang in my ears.

Home. Said as though the house were ours.

Out on the streets, I had a reputation. Sweet as sugar when unprovoked, but if you pissed me off, my retribution would rain down on you. Gang members who'd accidently clipped me, as well as a few idiots who'd purposefully attacked me, could vouch for this.

I grabbed the handle above my seat and hoisted myself up.

The Executioner swiveled to face me. "What are you—"

My foot snapped out, connecting with his temple. He grunted as his skull cracked against the window. The car jerked, veering close to the edge of the road.

He roared. "Woman, you are mad!"

I swung onto his lap, squeezing myself between his body and the steering wheel. "You're only just figuring this out?" As I spoke I cocked my arm back, and then I slammed it forward.

The Executioner caught my fist before I could land the blow, trapping it in his much larger hand.

With his other, he steered us to the side of the road. Once the car idled, he squinted at me. I breathed heavily, and I'm sure my eyes were dilated.

"You could've killed us," he said, his voice still raised.

"I could've killed *you*," I corrected. I'd already proved what happened to me when I got into a car accident.

The Executioner drew in a breath and stared at the fist he palmed, clearly still fascinated by the fact that he couldn't hurt me.

I tried yanking my hand away. "Let. Me. Go."

His lips twitched. "Then beg."

"Fuck you, I will not beg."

His grip on my hand transformed from punishing to tender. Rather than releasing me, he tugged on the hand, bringing me closer to him until my entire torso pressed flush against him.

His eyes trained on my mouth. "Beg."

"No."

He tilted his face down, and his nose brushed against mine. The contact brought out a smile on the Executioner's face, transforming it from plain menacing to screw-me menacing. There was a difference, one my girly parts understood with perfect clarity.

"I can stay here all night," he said.

"Not with that rager you can't." I looked pointedly down at where my legs straddled him. Someone was happy to see me.

"Are you going to let me go?" I tugged on my captive hand to emphasize my point.

"Now that I've got you where I want you?" he asked, his free hand settling against my waist. "Doubtful." He grinned. I felt that grin all the way down to the base of my belly.

He's a horrible, evil person. Don't be one of those girls that forgives a guy his shitty personality just because he's gorgeous.

But he's broken. No one's ever given him the chance. Also, I love fixing broken things.

The Executioner watched me the entire time. After his

appraisal, he cocked his head. "You really are crazy, aren't you?"

I swung my free hand at him, which he also caught. "Ah, ah, ah. Use your words."

"Oh that's real cute coming from you, Mr. I-Fry-People-for-a-Living." I tried to jerk my fists from his hold. No success.

Not even my words could wipe away the Executioner's perky mood. And I do mean *perky*.

"I'll tell you what," he said. "I'm feeling giving, so I'll let you go on the condition that you sleep with me."

I let out a laugh. The *cojones* of this man! "You let me go and I might not throat punch you."

"Yes, because you had so much success with that already." He squeezed my hands just to rub a little salt in the wound.

I growled out my frustration.

"Use your words," he reminded me.

"You can take your words and shove them up—"

The Executioner was done talking. His lips crashed into mine, and my words died in my throat.

"Gah, you are so smug." I stared daggers at the Executioner from the passenger seat. Eventually he'd let my hands go after we ... *discussed* things a bit more. We'd come to an agreement of sorts. One that he thought benefitted him more than me.

A corner of his mouth lifted. So self-satisfied. I wanted to punt that smile off of his face.

"It's been a good day in a sea of bad ones," he said.

"You call this a good day?"

"I got to kiss an Angel—and she liked it."

I raised an eyebrow. So I kissed him back. Again. Like I said before, the dude was a good kisser. "I pity you if you think this is a good day."

He gave me a passing glance. "Unlike some people," he turned the car towards his house, "my average day isn't full of bunnies and free hugs."

"My life isn't full of *bunnies*." I didn't address the other part of his comment. I was a hugger.

He scoffed. *Scoffed.* Motherfucker was so getting payback. He'd better sleep with one eye open.

"It's *not*."

The Executioner pulled into his garage and killed the engine. I followed him out of the car.

"I'm going to sleep well tonight because tonight, I'll be getting one of those famous free hugs of yours."

And that was the little agreement we came to. Same bed, no sex, lots of cuddling. Like I said, motherfucker better sleep with one eye open.

I narrowed my eyes at him. Even if he weren't a super-villain, he'd still be the most infuriating man I'd met. At least the most infuriating man who'd insisted we keep in each other's company.

We entered his house, and I found myself back in the confusing labyrinth of Mirage's illusions. It didn't help that five seconds after I entered the Executioner's house, I rammed my hip against the sharp corner of some invisible object.

I cursed, holding my side as my body healed itself.

"Be careful," the Executioner admonished, "that table's over two hundred years old."

Breathe in, breathe out. Don't throttle him ... yet.

"Next time I'll make sure to get out of the invisible table's way," I gritted out.

"If you need help maneuvering my home, you only have to ask." He took my hand, like the white knight he wasn't, and led me down the hall.

He took us to his kitchen. "Hungry?" he asked, letting my hand go to head towards the fridge.

"Oh really Master? Feeding the slave, Master? How gracious of you!"

"You want to talk about slavery? How about this: I have lived my life enslaved to my power. I will not be so anymore."

"So instead you kidnap me."

He ran his hands through his hair. "Woman, you're making this so difficult."

"My. Name. Is. Not. Woman."

He tore his hands from his face, his dark eyes stormy. "You can stay in my house as my captive or my girlfriend. You choose—"

I gasped. "Are you—are you asking me out?" I clasped my hands together. "I bet girls have just about *died* for the honor!"

The Executioner worked his jaw in annoyance. "Either way, you and I *will* get to know each other."

"You might as well just say it." I folded my arms and leaned against a counter as I spoke. "*Sex. Knocking boots.*

Hiding the sausage. Screwing. Making love. Or," I eyed him, "in your case, *fucking*. Definitely fucking." He had so much anger. I couldn't imagine anything less with him.

Abruptly the Executioner's attention shifted away from me, his gaze trained on the counter. His muscles tensed. My eyes flicked from him to the unoccupied surface, then back to him.

"Something amiss?" I asked. The words had only just left my mouth when a blast of icy air slammed into me, throwing me against the far wall. My head and shoulder smashed through plaster.

You know what? Screw this day.

The unnatural wind pushed upwards, wrenching my body from the plaster and forcing me up the wall. At least from this vantage point I was able to survey the room. At the far end, where the living room was, stood the man responsible for the wind. His hand jutted out at me, but even without that obvious gesture, I'd still recognize his scarred face.

Hurricane. Another one of the Cruel Countess's minions here to do her bidding.

Spread around him were Torment, who could influence with his words, Mirage the illusionist, and Chameleon, who could climb just about any surface and blend into his surroundings at will. Unfortunately, this latter power required complete nudity, and the man took advantage of it. Frequently.

At least he wore pants at the moment.

I'd never been around so many supervillains at once, and I had to say, it felt like bringing a knife to a gunfight.

The Executioner didn't move, but his muscles tensed.

"Still your idea of a good day?" I asked him.

He stared down the villains. "Fun's only getting started, Angel."

CHAPTER 14

Executioner

"Could've called before you invited yourselves into my home." I kept my voice even.

Hurricane tilted his head. "So you'd have time to escape with the girl? I don't think so."

They already knew I'd gone rogue. The Cruel Countess must've figured it out after our call. God knows she had the resources to do so.

"Hey fuckface," Angel said, "I went through puberty a decade ago. It's 'woman,' thankyouverymuch."

Now she was okay with "woman." Confusing female.

Hurricane raised his brows at me, a smile playing on his face. "*She* was the one that broke you?"

Yes, and I hate how desperate she's made me.

"You have ten seconds to leave my home," I said, my gaze touching each one of them. "Then, friend or not, I will kill you." I was girding myself for that reality. Angel and I wouldn't be getting out of this without spilling some blood.

"The Cruel Countess knows." Hurricane's eyes softened with pity.

Bzzzz ... bzzzz ... bzzzz ...

My phone vibrated in my pocket.

"Answer it," Hurricane ordered.

I retrieved the phone, the Cruel Countess's face lighting up the screen.

I accepted the call and put the cell to my ear.

"Hello, X."

"Countess."

"A little birdie told me you'd taken your work home with you."

I had nothing to say to that.

"This was to be a routine extraction," the Cruel Countess said. "Now it's not, and I'm losing money because you had a change of heart.

"You will be punished for this insurrection," she continued. "The longer you withhold Angel, the steeper the price you'll pay.

"That is all—oh, and X? Don't ever fucking *think* of crossing me again. I'll know."

The line went dead. My grip tightened on the phone, the plastic cracking. A shout built up in my throat, but I forced it back down.

Thank God I was in my hometown. I'd need to make

certain arrangements while I was here. Soon Angel and I wouldn't be the only ones on the run.

"You know what has to be done, X," Hurricane said. "Are you and the girl prepared to come quietly?"

I glanced up at Angel, who was still pinned to the wall. Would she be ready to act when shit hit the fan?

High above me she waited, looking bored and haughty despite the fact that our lives were on the line. Her eyes met mine, and I saw steely resolve. Damn me, my opinion of her just increased. She'd pull through.

"Yes." The word burned coming out. I made it a habit not to compromise; doing so now chafed, despite the fact that I planned to attack once the opportunity presented itself.

Hurricane nodded. "Torment, Chameleon, bring the van around."

They hesitated, I'm sure understanding that their absence left us evenly matched, and that was a dangerous thing, no matter how incapacitated Angel and I were.

"Now."

It took them several minutes to find the front door. As soon as it clicked shut, Hurricane eased up on the wind, gently lowering Angel to the ground. Both she and I wore identical, confused expressions.

"We're letting you go," Mirage said, stepping aside.

I loosened my muscles. "Why?" They owed me no allegiance.

"Because you alone can kill her." Hurricane didn't need to clarify whom he was referring to. The Cruel Countess was a menace to heroes and villains alike.

That was questionable.

"She'll know you helped us," I said.

"When we're questioned," Hurricane said, "we'll tell them you attacked us and got away with the girl."

"Not a girl," Angel reminded him.

He gave her a look that plainly said he was reconsidering freeing her.

I glanced over at Angel. "You going to cooperate?"

She folded her arms over her chest. "Only as much as usual." Difficult, infuriating woman. Of course the one person who could resist my touch would be my equal and opposite in so many ways.

I nodded to Hurricane and Mirage and strode out of the room, figuring Angel would follow. A glance over my shoulder proved that she was, in fact, sauntering behind me.

"Hey, X," Hurricane called out, "put on some goddamn gloves. You're going to inadvertently kill the girl."

He didn't know I could touch her. It wouldn't take them long to figure out—maybe the Cruel Countess already had—exactly why I'd never deliver Angel to them.

Angel

WE PEELED OUT of the Executioner's driveway just as the van pulled around the corner. Next to me, the Executioner reached into the side console. He came away with a Desert Eagle.

"A gun?" Derision dripped from my voice. "You can kill people with your touch and yet you carry a gun? I'm judging you."

He rolled down the window, flashing me a look before aiming the weapon at the van. "Hand-to-hand combat is overrated," the Executioner said.

I winced when he fired off two shots. I couldn't help it; I healed for a living.

The glass of the van's front window spider-webbed as the bullets entered. Blood sprayed inside. A moment later the car swerved across the road.

I tensed. "Are they dead?"

"Doubt it," he said, steadying his hand once more. "A supervillain will live long enough to carry out a vendetta."

That, I could attest to.

The Executioner shot at the car's front tire. Rubber split away from metal, and the van lurched as it peeled away from the vehicle, leaving the bald rim to spark against the asphalt.

The van came to a shuddering halt ahead of us.

I stared at the Executioner for a second. He wore the face of a torturer—calm and unaffected. Like he hadn't just possibly killed one of his associates.

He swerved to pass the stalled van.

A bullet tore through the window, and I felt the air shift as it whizzed by. I clutched my temple. "Holy mutha-effing unicorns and leprechauns," I said. "Those two better be glad they hadn't hit me. I get mean when I get shot."

Aiming behind us, the Executioner fired off the rest of the round. "If they caught us, bullets would be the least of your worries."

I didn't doubt it. The Executioner was renown for being the killer of superheroes, the Cruel Countess's most loyal and brutal weapon, and this was how she rewarded his first slip up.

The Executioner revved the engine, and his sleek sports car careened down the mountain. We passed by his abandoned Lotus. He didn't spare it a glance.

"Your boss sounds real nice," I commented when the silence stretched on.

"She's not my boss." The hood, which I was so used to the Executioner wearing, was down, and his hair dusted his cheekbones. Gorgeous man.

Wicked man.

"Then what is she?"

"A captor of sorts."

I peered at him, noticing his troubled look. "You mean to tell me that someone can control *you?*"

He glanced over, eyeing me up and down. "Anyone can force another's cooperation with the right incentives."

"And how does one incentivize the Executioner?" I asked, propping my feet up on the dashboard. "Promise him healers?"

"In case you didn't notice back at my place,"—his eyes flicked to my feet—"I diverged from script. I was supposed to hand you over to the Countess. I didn't."

He fell silent as we turned onto another street.

"She leverages loved ones to control supers," he finally said.

A nightmare situation.

My eyes widened as his words sunk in. "You have family?"

The Executioner gave a jerky nod. "In this very city."

"They live in L.A.?" Another surprise.

"I grew up here," he admitted. When I continued to stare at him, he elaborated. "I left, they lingered."

"And the Cruel Countess knows where these relatives live."

A frown. "Unfortunately."

"You fear she's going to use them against you."

The Executioner took a hand off the steering wheel to rub his chin. "*Him*—there's only one. And I know she will."

Even after divulging this information, the Executioner stayed calm and collected.

That's what it must take to live the life of a supervillain. Never showing weakness.

"Do you have a safe house your relative can go? Someplace strong enough to keep the Cruel Countess out?" I asked.

Silence. Then, "I'll drag him along with us," he said.

Us. Crap, this guy was going to haul me around while this all went down. Not to mention his relative. That was a very bad idea.

"I have a proposition for you," I said.

The Executioner eyed me up and down, a brow arched. "Whatever it is, I'm game."

I rolled my eyes. "Listen Don Juan, you and me are not happening." So long as my legendarily weak will power held out.

CHAPTER 15

Angel

WE PULLED UP to a rundown apartment complex in Westwood, both of us scrutinizing the area for signs of the enemy. Around us, teenagers and twenty-somethings congested the pavement and bike lanes, most wearing backpacks.

"Does your family member go to school at U.C.L.A.?" I asked, watching several students as they passed. We were less than a mile from the university.

Next to me, the Executioner nodded.

I still couldn't get over the fact that I had spent a day with *the* Executioner, one of the world's most dangerous and infamous supervillains. Even more surprising, neither of us had managed to kill the other.

Not that we hadn't tried.

"How long has it been since you last saw him?" I asked, turning my attention to the apartment.

Being a super—hero or villain—meant that you had to bury your past. That was why all of Los Angeles's super-heroes lived in one house. It wasn't like any of us picked our ridiculous names for the fun of it. Pasts and private lives could and would routinely be exploited. All of us had someone who meant something to us. The deeper those details were buried, the better. Otherwise crazies like the Cruel Countess would *incentivize* us all to do their bidding.

The Executioner—or X, as I was starting to refer to him in my head—drummed the steering wheel. "Too long— over a decade since we last saw one another."

"Did you leave on good terms?"

He appeared impatient, but I'd bet he was nervous. The Executioner had to be worried that this family member might be terrified of him.

"He saw me kill our father."

THE EXECUTIONER UNBUCKLED his seatbelt.

"Whoa, whoa, whoa amigo," I said, placing a hand on his chest. A man who'd committed patricide. In front of his brother.

Just when I was beginning to think of him somewhat decently ...

The Executioner's dark eyes flashed, and within them I saw both a killer and a wounded creature. The most dangerous combo.

"Ease up. I'll get your brother," I said.

"And chance you two running?" he said. "I think not."

Damn. It had been worth a shot.

"So," I said, "you were just planning on showing up after ten years and convincing your brother to leave with *you*, the notorious Executioner? Me thinks that won't end well."

"I managed to get you in the car with me."

My eyebrows hiked up. "So you're planning on kidnapping him? Oh hell no." I unbuckled my seatbelt and got out of the car. I was so not letting this guy threaten and manhandle his own brother.

I marched purposefully towards the building. Arms snaked behind me, and then the brilliant blue sky swam across my vision as the Executioner hauled me over his shoulder.

"If we do this," he growled, "we do this together. No running."

"You have three seconds to put me down, or it's goodbye to your gonads."

A moment later my feet touched the ground. Big surprise. You threaten the royal jewels and suddenly men get real cooperative.

I followed the Executioner up to the third floor, and we stopped in front of Apartment 6A.

My gaze moved over the Executioner, his dangerous hands shoved deeply into his pockets. He'd pushed his hood back over his face as soon as we were inside the building, and now his hulking frame loomed behind me.

"I better do the introductions," I said, stepping up to

the door.

The Executioner grunted.

I pounded on the door.

After several seconds I heard shuffling on the other side of the door. The footsteps paused while someone likely gazed through the peephole.

A moment later the door swung open. A handsome twenty-something eyed me up and down, looking both shocked and wary. Superhero house visits usually got these types of mixed reactions; we went where trouble lurked, after all.

"Hi," I said, "are you … ?" I'd never caught the brother's name.

"Marc," the Executioner supplied.

Marc glanced beyond me at the man who'd spoken, and his whole body froze as he took in the dark figure leaning against the hallway wall.

"*Sam?*"

Sam is an All-American boy, the kind of untroubled, attractive guy who also happens to be genuinely nice. Sam is a *good* guy. Sam is not a stone cold killer. Sam is not *the Executioner.*

"*Sam?*" I raised my eyebrows as I turned to the Executioner. "Really? Never would've guessed that one."

Marc stumbled back, his gaze drawn first to the Executioner's hooded face, and then down to his exposed hands. "What are you doing here?" Fear had threaded its way into his voice.

"Time for a reunion, brother," X said. "You're coming with us."

I rolled my eyes at the Executioner. "You really need to work on easing people into—"

Apartment door 6A swung closed as a frightened Marc tried to shut us out. Reflexively my foot snapped out to catch the door before it latched. It slammed into my foot and I suppressed a yelp.

The Executioner's palm slapped against the door, pushing it wide open. Behind it stood a pale-faced Marc. "I'm done waiting," X growled. "Out. Now."

MARC SLUMPED IN the backseat of the Executioner's car. "You can't just kidnap me," he said sullenly. Someone had already accepted his fate.

The Executioner had in fact threatened to touch Marc if he didn't cooperate. That got the morning moving along quite well.

"Your brother's an asshole," I said to Marc, "but, in his defense, for once he's actually trying to help."

"Help with what? He kills people for a living! Why drag me into it? And why are *you* with him?"

"Good question." I swiveled to face the Executioner. "*Sam*, care to explain this one?"

The Executioner's hands tightened on the wheel. "No."

I leaned over the seat. "Essentially, Marc, your idiot brother works for a bad woman, and he pissed her off when he kidnapped me—"

"I saved your life," X growled.

I swatted his shoulder. "Only after you tried to char-broil me from the inside out!"

"Wait," Marc interrupted, his gaze darting back and forth between X and me, "he tried to kill you, then he kidnapped you, and now you're working alongside him?"

"It's complicated," I said, staring at the Executioner.

The car fell silent.

"I still don't understand how I'm involved," Marc said, leaning forward. "Sam doesn't even care about me."

The Executioner white-knuckled the steering wheel, his mouth pressed into a thin line. "I do care," he said gruffly, his voice low.

"Then why did you disappear out of my life—no calls, no texts, nothing? I haven't heard from you in over a decade!" Marc ran a hand through his close-cropped hair, hair that was dark like his brother's. "I didn't even know you were alive until—" His voice caught in his throat. "When your victims started to appear. They died just like Dad."

I so did not want to be here right now.

"You know," Marc continued, "I don't hold you responsible for killing the mean bastard. *He* attacked *you*—you and I both know that. What I can't forgive is that you became just like him."

So the Executioner hadn't sought to kill his father after all. That made a difference.

The Executioner made a guttural noise, like a creature in pain. One look at him, and I knew he wasn't going to say anything. No explanation to the one person that actually deserved it. Coward.

"Listen, Marc," I said, rotating in my seat to face him,

"I'm going to tell you this because it needs to be known. Your brother never contacted you because he wanted to keep you safe. All supers have to cut ties for their family's protection."

"Then why am I in a car with you two?" If Marc looked worried before, now he appeared positively alarmed.

"Er—yeah, about that. Remember how I mentioned that your brother works for a bad woman, and that he pissed her off?"

Marc gave me a reluctant head nod.

"Well, she knows who you are and where you live."

The Executioner's brother groaned and leaned back in his seat. We'd saved his life, but we'd also messed it up.

I snuck a glance at X, who was as stoic as ever. All those charred bodies and superhero disappearances over the last two years—I'd seen them as senseless evil perpetrated by a crazed supervillain. Never had I guessed that all that horror was because someone had held a loved one against him.

How had this man survived when the world hated him? When even his own brother was more resentful than happy to see him?

My chest tightened.

"When will I be able to go home?" Marc asked, interrupting my thoughts.

"About that." I leaned over the headrest. "Marc, I've got a serious question for you: how would you like to stay in MadCap Mansion?"

CHAPTER 16

Angel

I COULD HEAR shrieking from somewhere in the house, then the sound of glass shattering.

Ah, home sweet home.

I barged into the entryway. "I'm ba-ack!" I sing-songed.

X had hated this idea—bringing his brother into his enemies' home. But he knew this was his brother's best option. My teammates would defend Marc with their lives if it came down to it.

Footsteps padded out from the kitchen. Shadow came into my line-of-sight, a carton of ice cream cradled in her arms and a spoon in her mouth. She pulled out the spoon, and threw her arms up into the air.

"My baby's home!" she yelled. Only after the words

were out of her mouth did she notice the two men behind me. "Oh shit. What is *he* doing here?" Her form started to disappear, until I could see the living room beyond.

"The Executioner's brother needs asylum."

"What the—?" A lighting bolt was already out of Zeus's hand before he'd fully entered the room, heading right for the men behind me.

I lunged directly in front of the bolt. It slammed into my chest, knocking me to the ground. My back arched and my body convulsed as the electricity pulsed through me. The nerve endings throughout my body screamed as they fried.

Holy fuck, this hurt.

My pulse pounded in my ears. *Thump–thuummp–thuuuumm* ... For one horrifying second my heart seized up. I gasped for air like a fish out of water, my eyes wide.

In the silence, I heard the Executioner's roar, and beneath that, the pound of footfalls and shouts.

... *mp–thump-thump.* I gasped as my heart restarted. The white noise began to distinguish itself.

"Angel, you idiot—"

"Zeus, I'm going to kill you—"

"Why is the Executioner in our house—"

"Dude looks PO'd—"

"*I will make you all pay.*"

Now, *that* voice I definitely recognized.

I heard the ominous sound of X's boots as he crossed the foyer. He passed me, his shoulders rolling as he stalked forward, his jaw set.

I sat up and rubbed my chest, my body sore everywhere.

At least it fared better than my suit. The material was now blackened and singed where the lighting bolt had struck me. Not even the L.A.S.D.'s seamstress would be able to mend this trainwreck.

My teammates stood at the opposite end of the foyer, their stances tense—all except Rocket, who hovered near the ceiling, one of his signature javelins held at the ready. The Executioner headed straight for them.

The world's baddest supervillian in the same room as a bunch of superheroes, and I somehow thought they might all be able to play nice.

Well, this ain't awkward or anything.

"X, stop." My voice came out thin and weak.

"Why?" he said, keeping his back to me.

"Because they're my friends and we need their help."

"*We?*" Zeus repeated, his gaze moving from the Executioner—who had halted—to me. "You *can't* be serious."

I pushed myself to my feet, my body much less tender now. Hate getting electrocuted. "All you asshats, can you please chill? And X, honestly, threatening my teammates is not going to endear you to anyone," I said, uncaring that my suit now had a giant hole from where I'd been struck.

Rocket floated down in front of me. "Angel, have you lost your mind? This man kills supers."

"Of course he does. He already tried that on me. Didn't work."

A strange sort of silence fell over the superheroes once I spoke.

Madman began to sing, "Angel and X-ie, sittin' in a

tree. K-I-S-S-I-N-G." Someone elbowed him and whispered for him to shut up.

The Executioner purposefully turned his back on the superheroes and swaggered towards me. "We're going. It's not worth the effort."

I put a hand on his chest and gave him a meaningful look. "They can help."

I stepped away from him and towards my team. "X and I are currently at the top of the Cruel Countess's wanted list, and Marc," I waved to the man whose back was pressed into the front door, as though it might absorb him if he wished hard enough, "X's brother, really needs a place to stay until this whole thing blows over."

"You're the Executioner's brother?" Aries asked, sizing the man up.

Marc shifted his weight and gave a jerky nod.

"Fucking-A," Zeus said, shaking his head. "*Days of Our Lives* has less drama than we do."

"Ever play *Halo*?" Aries asked Marc.

"Um," Marc glanced around, "yes?"

"Sweet. The dude can stay."

"*He* can't," Rocket said pointing to the Executioner.

X smirked. "Like I'd want to linger." He folded his arms and leaned against the wall.

"We're not staying," I said. I'd already decided this before we'd arrived. I refused to be the reason the Cruel Countess rained down her wrath on the good people of LA.

"Where are you going?" Shadow asked, stepping forward. Since I left my family behind, Shadow and Zephyr had become the closest thing I had to sisters.

Now her gaze moved between the Executioner and me. Had we been alone, she would've twenty-questioned me.

I bit my lip. "I don't know."

I FLIPPED ON the light switch, illuminating my digs. Books and papers cluttered my desk, as did a leftover Slurpee and several Starbucks cups. Clothes covered my bed and the back of my chair.

Ah, room, how I missed thee.

I turned to shut the door, only to find the Executioner crowding the threshold. Zeus and the rest of the team were showing Marc his room, as well as the rest of the house. I'd left X in the main room, but clearly he'd followed.

I smirked. "Is someone uncomfortable being in a building full of superheroes?"

"A wolf is not uncomfortable amongst a flock of sheep." *But the sheep are.* He left that part unsaid.

X leaned against the doorframe. "You and I need to talk."

I waved a hand to my bed, which was littered with clothes. "Make yourself at home."

The Executioner sauntered into the room, his body grazing mine as he passed. His attention moved to something above my bed, and I followed his gaze.

THIS RIDE WILL GET YOU WET.

I inwardly groaned. I'd swiped the cautionary sign from Disneyland a couple years ago. Thought I was oh-so-clever at the time.

I moved past the Executioner, grabbed another one of my dusted gold suits, and began shrugging off my singed one.

Now the Executioner's eyes snapped back to me, and there they lingered, getting more molten by the second.

I paused. "Can you not be so obvious about watching me undress?" Enough people had seen me naked that I wasn't prudish with this stuff, but to be so blatantly ogled …

The Executioner blinked, then moved farther into my room, inspecting my things.

"What is it you wanted to talk about?" I stepped into the new suit, wiggling it over my hips.

The Executioner lifted my lucky eight ball from the dresser and shook it. He frowned at whatever answer the eight ball gave him. "The Cruel Countess won't stop coming after us," he said, setting the ball down. "We can—"

"'*Fuck you, fuck you very very mu-u-uch,*'" Lily Allen sang from my phone, interrupting us.

The papers strewn over my desk muffled the sound somewhat. I pushed them out of the way.

"'*—uck you, fuck you very—*'"

I snatched the phone up. "Hello?"

"Oh, good, your sister said I would be able to reach you here," a husky female voice said.

A sensation I hadn't felt in a very long time now coiled itself low in my belly.

Fear.

My sister.

Impossible.

"You have the wrong number." Even as I spoke, the logic of my words curbed my fear. Of course it was the wrong number.

My eyes flicked up, and I met the Executioner's stare. His gaze held steady, but he rubbed his lower lip, his eyes narrowed.

"This is the correct number," the speaker's voice sounded distant, as though she turned to talk to someone, "isn't it, Ashley?"

"*No ...*" My hand began to shake.

And then it got worse, so much worse.

"A-Angel, p-please save me." Her voice came from somewhere beyond the speaker. I'd recognize it from anywhere.

It really was my sister.

I couldn't see the room I stood in so well. Not when tears blurred my surroundings. I clutched the phone tighter. Suddenly, the Executioner was in front of me.

"Do I still have the wrong number?" the woman clipped the words out.

"What do you want?" I asked.

"Oh, honey, I want so many things it would make your head spin. At the moment though? You, the Executioner, and a healthy dose of revenge. And I do plan on getting all three. We'll see in what order."

"Whatever you want from me, I'll give it to you. Just let my sister go."

X snatched the phone from my grip. I yelped when I realized it was gone and now I had no way—short of wres tling this bear of a man—to negotiate my sister's freedom.

"Fuck you, Countess," the Executioner said, putting the phone to his ear. I made a grab for it, but he simply placed a hand against my chest, effectively keeping me away. "You want to make deals, you go through me."

"You." I jumped and tried to snag the phone. A miss. "Won't." Jump. "Make." Jump. "Any." Jump. "Deals." Jump. "For me. Now give me back my phone."

The Executioner's eyes flicked to me. The asshole had the audacity to place his finger to his lips, like I was the problem here. "Then kill the girl," he said. "What do I care?"

"NO! No-no-no-no-no!" I began punching the Executioner in the arm, nice meaty slugs that did absolutely nothing to shake his hold of the phone.

"Angel is staying with me. End of story."

Click.

I stared at the phone dumbly. "You just hung up. You told the Cruel Countess to kill my sister, and then you hung up." My gaze moved up to the Executioner.

Without warning, I lunged at him. "You sick, son-of-a-bitch, I will end you!"

The Executioner caught me, and together we fell onto my mattress.

X pinned me down on the bed. "Would you simmer down, woman, and let me talk?"

"She's going to die and it's all your fault!"

"I took your sister off the table as leverage. So long as the Cruel Countess thinks she has power over you—"

"She does!"

"—she'll be able to call the shots. If she thinks I won't let you retrieve your sister, she won't be as eager to use her against you."

That ... made sense.

Still.

"You told the Cruel Countess to kill her!"

"And right now," he spoke slowly, "your sister is of more use to the woman alive. I've worked closely with the Cruel Countess. I know her strategy. She's still planning on capturing you, and once she does, she'll use your sister again—for leverage and revenge."

When I stopped fighting him, the Executioner released my wrists. I sat up and pushed a hand through my hair. Took a deep breath. "Then there's only one thing left to do."

The Executioner nodded. "We're going to have to take the Cruel Countess down."

CHAPTER 17

Angel

I GRABBED A duffle bag from my closet then began dumping clothes into it at random. I paused. "Where, exactly, does the Cruel Countess live?"

"Miami."

"Miami," I repeated. The hours stretched out in front of me—the drive to the airport, the flight, the time it would take to locate my sister and decide on a plan of action.

An eternity. Ashley could die at any point before then.

I threw clothes into my bag with more vigor; I *hated* feeling helpless.

As far as cities go, Miami wasn't a bad place to kick ass and take names. I shoved in two swimsuits—one for me and one for my sister. I would be getting her back damn it, and before I had to whisk myself from her life once more, I'd be having a beach day with her.

Time to cash in my good karma points.

Executioner leaned against the wall closest to my window and watched me pack with cool detachment.

"We need to go," he finally said.

"Almost finished."

I knelt next to my bed and dragged out a thin case that was wider and longer than my luggage. Unfastening the clips on either side, I flipped the lid up. Nestled inside were knives, guns, and throwing stars. I strapped some of them on and piled others into my duffle. Once I was done, I closed the case once more and slid it back under my bed.

I zipped up my luggage and grabbed my fishbowl. "I think I'm ready," I said.

The Executioner raised an eyebrow. "The fish can't come."

"I'm not leaving Chub-Chub behind."

His mouth twitched. "It's ... a fish. How attached can you be to a creature that will die in a month?"

I glared at him. "We're a package deal."

The Executioner let out a long-suffering sigh. "We're boarding a plane. Does ..." another lip twitch, "Chub-Chub travel well?"

I stared down at my fish, frowning. Inside the bowl, he wobbled with the water, his eyes wide, silently begging me to put him down. A plane flight would be hellish on the little guy.

"Perhaps he could face off against the Cruel Countess?"

X asked, now clearly enjoying himself. "It would save us the trouble."

I sighed and set the bowl on my desk. Grabbing a pen and a piece of paper, I scribbled feeding and bowl cleaning instructions and taped the note to my doorknob for Shadow, who chronically visited my room to borrow clothes. She'd feed him until I came back.

If I came back.

"Are you ready?" X asked.

I took one final look around my room. I'd lived here for the majority of my adult life and I couldn't help but get a little sentimental. I had no idea when I'd see it again.

Finally, I nodded. "Let's go."

Executioner

I DROVE US to the airport, spending part of the drive coordinating a flight to Miami.

Next to me, Angel jiggled her leg, no doubt thinking about her sister.

The Cruel Countess threw a wrench in my plans. I'd been ready to run. To cash in all of my favors and disappear with Angel. It might've worked too, but now it wouldn't.

Instead we were set on a suicidal quest to take out the most powerful supervillain alive.

... Or at least that was what Angel assumed we were doing.

Need to hide her so deep the Cruel Countess will never find her.

Even that would be problematic. I'd already admitted that the Cruel Countess lived in Miami.

Fool.

Now I'd have to tow Angel along with me and pretend I was all for this idiotic plan.

Did she even know just how powerful the Countess was? Had she ever wondered why so many superheroes had disappeared? Or noticed that superheroes weren't the only ones that went missing? Supervillains had vanished into thin air as well.

I was going to have to lie to this woman and betray her trust. Not the first time I'd ever done this, but now it didn't sit well with me. And just when something in her eyes changed when she looked at me.

Damn you Countess for making me both more altruistic and more despicable than I ever intended to be.

I only hoped that at the end of it all Angel realized I did what I did to save her.

Angel

WEAPONS CLANKED AGAINST me as we approached the Executioner's jet.

Already I was regretting not asking any of my teammates to join us. I was insane to think that I could take down the Cruel Countess by myself.

Well, not entirely by myself.

Even carrying our bags, X still managed a mean swagger. He knew the Cruel Countess far better than I did, and he was ready to take her down.

He climbed up the staircase ahead of me. The stewardess standing up at the entrance kept her expression pleasant as he passed, but I saw her step away from him.

I followed him inside, my eyes widening as I took in the jet's interior. "This is all yours?"

X busied himself with stowing our luggage. "I can't exactly board a commercial airliner."

No, I suppose he couldn't.

"Sit," the Executioner said, nodding to a table and set of seats that surrounded it. "We have much to discuss."

I headed over and plopped down into one of the leather seats. Drumming my hands on the table between us, I said, "Hit me with it."

X slid into the seat, and his attention moved from my face to my hands. He removed his jacket and shrugged off his gloves. Only once he'd set them aside did he begin to speak.

"How much do you know about the Cruel Countess?" he asked.

"Not much," I admitted. Only that the witch had my sister.

"That's what I thought."

He leaned forward, bracing his forearms on the table. "Amongst supervillains we have a saying: it's the ones you know the least that you should mind the most. There's a reason no one knows anything about her, even though she controls organized crime along the eastern seaboard, the Gulf, and the Caribbean. People should be sprouting up all over the country with stories on her."

The hair on my forearms rose. X reached out and ran his hand along my gooseflesh. The skin smoothed out under his touch.

Those dark eyes peered into mine. "Do you know what her ability is?"

I shook my head. Something in the Executioner's gaze made my stomach plummet.

"She can steal others' abilities."

He gave me time to digest that. When it sank in, my blood ran cold.

The missing superheroes.

"How many has she stolen?"

"Dozens, maybe hundreds. She's old, though you wouldn't know it."

"Hundreds?" I repeated weakly. The woman who held my sister might've siphoned away hundreds of powers. "What happens to her victims?"

The Executioner's mouth pressed into a frown. It was all the answer I needed.

Death.

"And the stolen powers—how long can she use them for?" I asked.

"When she takes another's ability, it's for good."

"So at this very moment she can wield—at will—every power she's stolen."

X's jaw tightened. "Yes."

An army contained in a single woman. And we were

heading straight for her.

CHAPTER 18

Angel

SOMEONE GENTLY SHOOK my shoulder. "Angel, we're here."

I blinked my bleary eyes, confused by my surroundings. The white leather, the cool, recycled air, the man bending over me.

Then my situation slammed into me. The Executioner. The Cruel Countess.

My sister.

I pushed off the blanket someone had draped over me and scrambled up. The Executioner wore the same grim expression I wore—minus the panic.

I had too much energy; my legs jittered with the need to run.

Have to save my sister. Have to save my sister. I took a deep breath. Careening headlong into battle was a great way to get killed, especially if the Cruel Countess was just as deadly as X made her out to be.

As soon as I stepped off the jet, a wave of humid heat hit me. Give it an hour, and this suit would proudly display rings of armpit sweat.

The Executioner followed behind me.

"Don't tell me you have digs here?" I said, glancing over at him. We hadn't discussed sleeping arrangements. Normally when I traveled, I stayed with the city's supernatural department, but with a stowaway like the Executioner, I highly doubted they'd offer up their guest rooms.

X slid on a pair of glasses underneath his hood. Overkill, if you asked me.

"Of course," he said, watching a town car make its way towards us.

I would not be impressed by this man's wealth. I would not.

Thirty minutes later the driver deposited us in front of the Executioner's beachside mansion.

Okay, I was a little impressed.

"You are gawking at my house like men do breasts," the Executioner noted once we'd exited the car.

I blinked rapidly, refocusing my attention on the man sitting next to me. "Like you're one to talk about gawking," I said.

He grunted, pulling a key out of his pocket and heading up the driveway. The sky blazed pinks and oranges as the sun set.

"You're going to have to watch your step," he said as I

followed him up. "This house is also full of illusions.

I groaned. "Will you at least not lock me in the room this time?"

"So long as you don't try to escape."

Fat chance of that happening.

"I want food, then liquor, then bed. If you can give me those things, then I'm all yours."

The Executioner swiveled away from the door, an eyebrow arched. His eyes smoldered as he took me in, and I realized too late what I'd just said. "Done."

WHILE X WENT to set down our things, I ruffled my hair and headed into the kitchen. Opening his freezer, I saw frozen vegetables, meat, ice cubes ... and a bottle of Jack.

"Hello lovely. Come to mama," I said, reaching in. I unscrewed the top and gulped down a healthy swig before the Executioner came up from behind me.

His body pressed in close, and his hand brushed along the skin of my arm before he reached around me and snagged the bottle from my grip.

He was getting bolder with his touches and I was noticing them more. Something had changed between us since I helped him hide his sibling and he decided to help me retrieve mine.

He eyed me as he took a swallow of the whiskey, then capped the thing.

He nodded to the stools on the other side of the room. "Sit down. I'll make you a drink and a meal."

I bit the side of my lip. "Okay ..." What was I supposed

to make of this man? I could hate him when he was a criminal, but this was a bit harder.

Does he realize just how vulnerable he's been around me?

I slid into the seat as he began mixing me a drink, cutting up limes and squeezing them into two glasses. Then he chopped up mint and added it in.

"Who bought all the groceries?" I asked.

"One of my people," he responded.

Another mindboggling part of this man. He couldn't get close to others, but he had employees to see to his needs.

When he finished preparing the drink, he handed it over. I took it from him and pretended not to notice the slight tremor that worked through him when our fingers brushed.

"I still keep thinking I'm going to kill you every time I do that," he said.

"You can't get rid of me that easily."

He cracked a smile. "Good, I wouldn't want to."

We stared at each other for several seconds before I swallowed and lifted the drink to my lips. Anything to ignore the fact that my body was down to do the horizontal tango with his. Worse, I already knew he was game.

I took a sip of the drink he made, and my eyes widened. "That's good. What is it?"

"A mojito—and a peace offering," he said, pouring himself a shot of Jack.

I eyed him.

"I was hoping we could start over again." He brought the Jack to his lips, and heaven help me, watching this man drink should not be as erotic as it was.

"Hmmm," I said, taking another sip and considering him over the rim of the glass. "You tried to kill me, you kidnapped me, you threatened to kill my friends. Oh—" I snapped my fingers, "and you called me a psycho, which was just rude." I drank a little more. "I'm not sure I'm ready to play nice with you."

He worked his jaw, then nodded.

I waited for him to say more, but instead the Executioner pushed away from the counter and began to pull out food. Not much of a talker, this one.

"You could try saying you're sorry."

He glanced up, his eyes flashing. "I'm not."

Apparently that right there was a hot button. I'd really thought we'd begun to make a breakthrough too.

A muscle in his jaw jumped, and he turned his attention back to his work.

I watched him move around the kitchen. His hair hung over his face as he chopped vegetables, and my heartbeat sped up.

He caught me looking and his brows furrowed. "What?"

I shook my head. "Nothing." I glanced down at my drink. "What are you making?"

"Fish."

I pursed my lips and tried not to scrunch my nose. "Fish are friends, not food."

He looked at me like I was insane.

"You've never seen *Finding Nemo?*"

"Do I look like the kind of man that's seen *Finding Nemo?*"

"Point taken."

Once he finished preparing the fish, he slipped the fil-lets into the oven and leaned against the counter, folding his arms over his chest.

I swirled my drink around. "You like to cook?"

He shrugged a shoulder.

"Like to talk?"

He shrugged another shoulder.

"Wanna fuck?"

His head snapped to me.

"Oh, *that's* a yes—maybe some other time."

He growled and stalked over to me. Gripping the count-er on either side of me, he leaned in. "You'd do well not to toy with me."

And just like that, I ruined my panties. Only now was I discovering that I had a thing for bad guys. Or at least this one. And I thought Shadow was the one with the bad boy problem.

I reached up and tugged on one of the loose locks of hair that dangled in front of his face. "But you're so *fun* to toy with."

He caught my hand, but when his skin met mine, he hesitated to release it. Mere inches separated our faces. Just like before, his annoyance faded, replaced by a rising heat. This intense man was drowning in his own needs. To touch and be touched. I could see it written onto his face.

Like a wildfire, that need spread to me, burning, con-suming until I could no longer fight it.

I don't know who moved first, but suddenly his lips

were hot on mine. His hands cupped my face, bunching my hair as he did so. He kissed me hard, feverishly, our mouths desperate for one another. His tongue found my own, caressing it.

I ran my palms down his sides, feeling that hard packed muscle. What I wouldn't give to be closer to him. My hands glided over his hips, closing in on the top button of his pants.

His grip on me tightened.

Despite my words, we *could* do this right now. There was nothing stopping us except, except—

I broke off the kiss. "We need a plan," I gasped out, leaning my forehead against him. "A plan to save my sister." Even forgetting that, for a second, had guilt swamping my system.

X nodded against me, his hands reluctant to leave my hair. Finally, he backed away.

We stared at each other as he moved to the other side of the counter, putting a physical barrier between us. My body wept at the distance, at the lost opportunity.

"The Cruel Countess will be keeping her in the compound," X said. "The first task is to get into the building itself. That won't be an issue. What will be an issue is that there is no way to go in unnoticed. As soon as we get close, we'll be monitored."

I leaned my elbows on the counter and gazed at X's lips, still distracted by the kiss. "We'll have to pretend to turn ourselves in."

X nodded. "Our biggest hurdle will be getting close enough to the Cruel Countess to kill her."

How did one kill a supervillain that wielded a legion of powers? Especially when no one—hero or villain—had managed to do so up until now?

She's always had the advantage. The odds must be evened.

"What happens once we get close enough?" I asked, still musing over my thoughts.

"I touch her." A spark of excitement lit the Executioner's features. This man has a score to settle.

"She's not immune?"

He gave me a funny look. "She hasn't stolen a healer's powers. Yet."

Hence our current situation.

"Why would someone like the Cruel Countess want my power? Seems odd."

X took a long swallow of his Jack, then set it down. "She's a sick fuck. Likes to torture people for the thrill of it. My best guess? She wants your power so that she can draw out her torture sessions."

I drew lines on the frosted sides of my drink. "Is she ... really that depraved?"

X leaned against the other side of the counter. "Yes."

I pushed my drink away and stood. "We need to get my sister, X. Now."

I strode towards the door having no idea where I was going but knowing that if I didn't do something, I'd combust.

X jogged up behind me, caught my wrist, and spun me around. "Are you suicidal?" he demanded, his voice rising. "You can't just waltz in there and demand your sister. You and she will both die. Painfully."

"Well, I can't do this, either." Eat. Sleep. Waste time. I thought I could bear it, but the more I learned of the Cruel Countess, the more frantic I became.

"You *must* do this," X insisted, "torture or not. We get one shot, Angel. One shot. You want to blow it because you got restless?"

I blinked back the moisture in my eyes. "But she's my baby sister," I pleaded, already knowing the truth of his words.

X took both my hands and pressed them together. "I know," he said, squeezing my hands. "We will get her back," he said. "Even if it kills me, we will get her back."

CHAPTER 19

Executioner

ANGEL BEGAN TO cry thick, sobbing tears.

I'm a fucking fool.

Promising this woman that I'd get her sister back to her. I'd been digging my own grave from the moment I'd decided I wouldn't hand Angel over.

Even more horrifying, I didn't regret any of it. I would rather die trying to save Angel's sister than be the reason she lost her.

Pathetic.

I'd developed the dreaded savior complex so many superheroes had, and all it took was a little ... hope.

I still held Angel's hands in my own. Instead of pulling away from me, she leaned into my chest and buried her face into my shirt, her salty tears wetting the material.

My eyes had widened, like a horse spooked. This had never happened.

How does one deal with these creatures when they cry?

I knew what I did when I was upset—pounded my fists into flesh and exacted my revenge. And I'd already promised her revenge. She'd cried only *after.*

Perhaps another approach. What had I always longed for at my loneliest?

Touch. Connection.

Of course.

Fool.

Cautiously I brought my arms up and around Angel, waiting for the moment she'd push me away and tell me she didn't want a monster touching her.

It never happened.

She's in my arms. Accepting this. Accepting me. Ah, I could die like this.

Without thinking I leaned down and kissed the crown of her head, causing her to nestle even deeper into my chest, like she might burrow herself a home.

That was fine by me.

More than fine.

How the hell had I managed not to blow this already?

You will, X. Once she finds out your real plans, you will.

AFTER MY SOBFEST, X and I returned to the kitchen. I'd had his fish—delicious—and then I'd had his alcohol. Lots of his alcohol. Dulling my senses seemed to be the only way I wouldn't do something stupid or brash.

Not that I stayed inebriated for any impressive length of time; my power purged the stuff out of my system as quickly as possible.

I leaned back against the couch we'd moved to, which was two feet to the left of where its illusion was. I'd slung my legs over X's lap, enjoying the brief panic in his eyes before he figured out what the appropriate reaction was. There was something innocent and alluring in that ignorance.

"So, what's the story with you and the Cruel Countess?" I asked, wiggling my toes.

He swirled the tumbler of Jack in his hand. "She found my brother and used him to gain my cooperation."

Know how that feels.

He took a deep breath and settled against the couch. He rubbed his mouth, his eyes growing distant. "The Cruel Countess had been trying to recruit me for a long time. Before I worked for her, I'd been a gun for hire. Believe it or not, it was almost always the good guys that hired me, usually to take out arms dealers, terrorists, and the like."

One of his legs began to jiggle. "I struggled with my power, with the anger and resentment I held towards others, but I never killed innocents. Not until ..."

The corners of his lips turned down. "When the Cruel Countess found out about my ability and my reputation, she wanted to hire me." X shook his head. "Easiest refusal I'd ever made."

This troubled man had fought his terrible ability; he'd tried to keep some shred of his humanity. It hurt to see that it had all been in vain.

"She kept coming back with bigger and bigger offers, until finally I told her, 'There is no price high enough to change my mind.'" He gave a hollow laugh. "That was my first lesson on the Cruel Countess—that she loves a good challenge.

"To this day I don't know how she'd found my brother. Only that she did. She sent me a stack of photos, all of Marc. Walking to class, grabbing food, in his bed asleep."

X closed his eyes, his brow creasing at the memory. "She'd found my price."

My legs stilled on his lap.

"For the last two years I never defied the Countess's orders, never gave her a reason to bring my brother back into the fray."

All those horrible things he'd done ... he'd been protecting his little brother. He'd sacrificed the last of his morality to do so.

"Not until now."

JUST WHEN I thought my story had scared her off completely, Angel clambered over me and pressed a soft kiss to my lips.

"I'm sorry," she said. And that was it.

I gave a gruff nod.

She crawled onto my lap, and curled up there. Perhaps she thought pressing herself close would somehow comfort me. My dick begged to differ. There was nothing comfortable about this at the moment.

Angel moved against me, and I bit back a groan.

She did it again, turning her head so that her nose brushed mine. "I'm tired," she said, her voice husky.

Was she hinting at sleep or sex?

She leaned in, her lips meeting mine.

Sex, definitely, sex.

Seal the deal. Make her yours. For the love of God, at least touch her.

My arms went around her. But while her fingertips smoothed down my chest, feeling everything, mine stayed in place.

What if I'm reading this wrong?

I broke off the kiss. "I'll show you your room."

I let out a sigh of relief when Angel untangled herself from my lap, despite missing the physical contact.

I was terrified of myself around her.

Because she already ran from me, just like everyone else. And why wouldn't she? I'd treated her like I did my hits. And in order to get her back, I threatened death on her friends.

But she also cried in my arms and took comfort from my touch.

I stopped in front of the bedroom door, anger replacing sadness. I could dismember a man without feeling a thing, but the mere thought of crossing boundaries I'd never crossed made me break out into a sweat. I needed to get a fucking grip.

As Angel shuffled into the room, she yawned once, then twice, her entire body shaking with the force of it. "I never thought your bed would look so good." She fell forward onto it, throwing her arms out as she hit the mattress like she was hugging it.

I remembered the sign above her bed at Madcap Mansion and my hard-on became downright painful. It didn't help that Angel looked cute as fuck with that dreamy smile on her face.

I hung back by the door. This strange, strange creature. Originally I found her antics annoying, but the longer I was around her, the more they grew on me.

Because she's mine. Mine.

Angel rolled over, her eyes flicking to my stance. I had one foot in the bedroom and one foot out. "You're not staying?" she asked, sitting up.

I paused. "Do you want me to stay?"

In response, a sly smile blossomed on her face. She reached her arm out for me.

Oh the temptation.

She was still torn up about her sister. And she'd cried on me. Took comfort from me. *Don't be the man that takes advantage of that.*

I dragged in a deep breath. "I need to make a call, but I'll be back."

She furrowed her brow at that, but nodded.

I left her there, heading back for the kitchen, where I poured myself another glass of Jack. I knocked it back and rubbed my eyes. Being halfway decent was harder than it looked.

I shifted my weight and groaned at my tight pants.

Definitely harder.

By the time I re-entered Angel's room, she was fast asleep.

I watched her slumbering form for a minute, her lips puckered. Without thinking, I headed over to her side, wanting to see an up close version of this Angel.

Rare to see her this quiet.

After a moment, I brushed a few strands of hair away from her face. She made a soft noise and leaned into the touch, her lips tilting up into a smile.

She couldn't be too much younger than I was, and yet I felt like I'd weathered lifetimes in whatever age gap separated us. Had she killed before? Even if she had, it wouldn't be like how it was for me—a necessary part of my life.

I moved to the couch and stretched out. She began to snore softly, dragging an unwilling smile to my lips.

I folded my arms over my chest and closed my eyes. I'd have to leave soon, but maybe, just maybe I could squeeze in a few hours of sleep near my Angel.

CHAPTER 20

Angel

I woke with a start, not aware of what had jolted me out of sleep. Outside, the soft glow of lamps trickled into my room.

Not *my* room—the Executioner's room. I was in Miami, staying with one of the world's most wanted criminals, and somehow, together, we were going to take down the Cruel Countess.

Across from me on the couch, the man himself lay stretched out, his arms and legs crossed, and his chin tucked against his chest. His eyes were closed. While most people looked calmer in sleep, he wore a frown.

Silly man, taking the couch when he could've joined me.

Out in the hall, a floorboard creaked. It could be the

house settling ... or it could be something else. I threw my covers off, thankful that I hadn't taken the time to remove my suit before I knocked out.

I padded to the door, leaned my back against the wall next to it.

Another creak, this one closer.

"X," I whispered.

His eyes snapped open, focusing on me immediately. There was no in-between with this man—one moment he was asleep, the next he was alert.

I tapped a finger to my ear, then to my mouth.

His gaze flicked to the door as he pushed off the couch. He headed towards the other side of it, his footsteps silent.

I grabbed the gun still holstered to my suit, bringing it up to my chest and glanced over at him.

He gave me a nod, and I breathed in, readying myself.

I stared at the brass doorknob, tensing when it began to turn. It stilled, and then the door edged open, allowing me to see out into the hallway beyond. In the darkness I made out a figure.

Reacting off training, my leg snapped out, landing solidly on a chest.

The figure stumbled back, and I followed him out into the hallway, cocking the gun and aiming it at his heart.

Shoot to kill. That was what my trainer had told me when I learned to use firearms. *If you aren't prepared to take someone out, then the gun shouldn't be in your hand in the first place.*

The gun shouldn't be in my hand. I wasn't prepared.

I began lowering the gun.

I don't want to kill this man.

X pushed past me and grabbed the man by the neck, hauling him to his feet as he began to scream. "Angel, keep the damn gun pointed," X said. "The Gambler here is not alone."

"The Gambler?" I'd heard of him because of how he'd earned his name, gaming casinos out of their money. He could persuade people to do things.

"He's one of the Cruel Countess's men," X said, studying the man with cool detachment.

Choking noises were replacing the man's screams. My aim drooped, and I watched in horror as something ate the man up from the inside out. His skin began to smoke, and the smell of burned flesh stung my nostrils.

Never had I witnessed the Executioner in action, and it was ... terrifying.

"Keep your gun up," X reminded me.

The Grambler's struggles slowed. X would kill him, right in front of me.

Making a decision, I dropped the gun to my side and touched the Gambler's bare skin. The man stopped struggling, and I could hear him catching his breath, as though he caught a brief respite from the pain. His skin was a mass of angry blisters and red, raw flesh.

"Angel, let go," the Executioner stated calmly.

"You're the one worried about a sneak attack. You let go."

X worked his jaw. "Woman, you drive me insane," he said, but he relented, releasing the man and backing away.

Gambler gasped as he collapsed onto the floor. I followed him down, keeping skin-on-skin contact. His flesh went from red to a dull pink, the exposed flesh healing over.

The Executioner snatched my hand away. "That's enough."

"Hey!"

"Heal him too much and he'll attack you all over again."

It was sound logic. I followed the same rule when healing a violent perpetrator who might otherwise die.

"But the damage ..." The Gambler's injuries were far too extensive.

The Executioner put a boot to the man's chest and stared him down. "If you so much as try to persuade Angel to help you, I'll finish what I started, and this time I'll take it real slow." He shoved his heel harder into the Gambler's chest before he stepped away.

He swiveled to me. "If you so much as think Gambler's trying to persuade you, shoot him." X glanced down the hall. "Other than that, don't do anything stupid and don't move. I'll be back." He pulled his own gun out of its holster and headed down the dark corridor.

Awesome. He'd determined that I was the rookie here, and he was my knight in shining armor.

"It's not like I've never done this before!" I yelled after X.

"So dumb," I whispered under my breath.

I leaned back against the wall. The smell of sizzled flesh still tinged the air.

"Can you even talk?" I asked the man at my feet.

"Uggggg," he moaned.

"Yeah, that's what I thought." I wouldn't be able to get

any information out of him like this. My hands twitched with the need to heal him.

Do that and you might miss your chance to save your sister.

Thoughts like that were the reason heroes cut ties with their family. Loved ones always had a little more currency than regular civilians.

I squatted down and reached a hand into the man's pockets. He moaned again as I jostled his sensitive skin.

"Would you quit being a baby?" I said. "If you behave, I'll heal you." Eventually.

He curbed his cries, and I began flipping through his pockets, looking for anything of use.

From one pocket I pulled out a wallet. Inside were a series of fake driver's licenses.

I clucked my tongue. "Identity theft is a mean crime."

I continued my search, whistling when I saw the amount of cash he carried. "Lot of hundreds in here. Still have that nasty gambling habit?"

The man whimpered. I set the wallet aside and finished patting him down. He wasn't even carrying a gun on him. Awfully optimistic to think he wouldn't need it.

I heard the squeak of a floorboard, and I began to look up.

Did I check the pockets on the Gambler's jacket? The thought drew my attention back down to the man.

I frowned. *Of course I did–*

A hand covered my mouth, and I felt the cool press of a gun barrel against my temple. "Cooperate and you'll be fine," the man whispered into my ear.

I should cooperate, shouldn't I?

I glared at the Gambler, fighting his compulsion.

Meanwhile, the man behind me let out a groan and rolled his shoulders. "Thanks," he whispered, tugging me backwards. "Old injury."

Well shit on a stick, I hated it when bad guys did that—used me to heal themselves against my will.

"Drop the gun," he ordered.

I bit my cheek, unwilling to do as he told me.

He shook me. "Drop it."

Reluctantly I let it go. The gun thumped loudly on the ground. The only thing I hated worse than being considered a rookie was actually feeling like one.

"Good girl. Let's go," he whispered.

He gave me a yank, and I stumbled forward, thoroughly pissed off. I might actually consider taking a bullet to the brain just to fight this guy.

A shadow appeared at the end of the hall.

X.

The man behind me must've seen him as well because he paused, giving me the opening I needed.

Using my right forearm, I knocked the gun away from my face.

Thwump. The bullet missed me by a hair, embedding itself into the hallway wall. The man had a silencer attached to the gun, making the whole thing sound much more harmless than it was.

Motherfucker tried to shoot me!

Down the hall, X roared, accompanying my rage.

I slammed my elbow back into the man's gut. As he folded over, I swiveled, planting a roundhouse kick to his temple. He went down, and I followed him to the ground. Arm cocked, swift follow-through. My fist crashed into his face, packing all my energy behind it.

Beneath my hand his nose crunched.

I pulled my fist back.

I didn't think this man was even a supervillain.

The Cruel Countess sent a regular criminal to bring me in. The gall.

No sooner had the thought crossed my mind, than my body levitated off the ground.

Telekinetic. I stared down at the man, surprised and a little impressed.

The Executioner brushed past me. My attacker lifted a hand, presumably to levitate the Executioner, but he moved a second too slow.

X's hands wrapped around the man's throat. Almost instantaneously the telekinetic began screaming.

His concentration broken, I fell, my teeth clicking together as my head thwacked the hardwood floor.

I moaned, pushing myself up. The Gambler had crawled down the hall, and like me, dude was taking a breather. I leaned against the wall and closed my eyes, clenching my teeth against the god-awful shrieking.

Him or my sister, I reminded myself.

By the time I stood up, X had dropped the smoldering remains of the man. I went to touch him.

"I wouldn't do that," the Executioner warned.

I did it anyway. Searing heat burned my flesh, and reflexively, my hand jerked back.

Dead.

X drew a knife from his pants' holster. "It was you or him, Angel," he said, his words closely aligning with my earlier thoughts. "I picked you."

My gaze locked on the knife. "What are you doing?"

"Are you ready to heal the Gambler?" X asked, heading past me.

I narrowed my eyes. "Only if you don't kill him."

"Oh, I won't do *that*," X said, and I could hear the ominous smile in his voice as he stared down at the man. The Gambler must've heard it as well, because he whimpered.

I sighed. "No wonder you suck at making friends. You're going about this all wrong." I headed after him.

"And Angel plays the good cop—big surprise there."

I rolled my eyes. "You so needed more hugs when you were a kid."

X grunted, not arguing. It reminded me that whatever tormented childhood he had, it had shaped him just as much as his power.

He crouched in front of the Gambler. "We're going to play a little game called 'I ask and you tell.' Every time I ask you a question, you answer honestly. Every time you do otherwise—and I'll know when you lie—I take off a finger.

"Simple rules. Got it?"

The Gambler nodded, then winced like the movement hurt him.

X leaned back on his haunches. "Okay, I'll start you off easy." He flipped the knife in his hand. "Who sent you here?"

The Gambler tracked X's movements. "The Cruel

Countess," he croaked.

"Good." The Executioner stopped flipping the knife. "What were her orders?"

The supervillain wheezed. "To capture Angel and bring her in."

X nodded. "And me? What orders did she give you about me?"

"She said she'd deal with your herself," he wheezed.

That knife flipped in the Executioner's hand, and he leaned forward. "Where is Angel's sister?"

My heart beat a little faster, and I inched closer, my legs nearly brushing against X's back.

"Who?"

"Mortal girl. Young. Captured within the last couple days. Insurance so that this one"—he hiked his knife back at me—"comes quietly."

"I have no idea, man—"

X grabbed the Gambler's shirt, which had partially fused to his skin and yanked him closer. An agonized scream ripped from the Gambler.

"You're lying." X shook his head. "You know the rules." He began reaching for the man's hand.

"No—no, please. I take it back—she's on the prison block. Last I heard the Countess hasn't torn into her."

I glanced away at that, breathing through my nose to control my rising emotions. *Torn into her?*

From my peripherals I saw X halt. "And?" he said.

"And what? That's all I know."

The Executioner reached for the Gambler's hand.

"Wait—wait man!" Fear threaded through his voice. "I

thought I answered your questions!"

"You did, but you still lied."

The man's panicked eyes locked on the Executioner. "Please!"

"X," I said. We had what we needed.

He stiffened, his grip tightening on the knife. Faster than my eyes could follow, X swiveled, the knife glinting as he turned it on me. The sharpened edge ripped through fabric and the skin of my abdomen.

I staggered backwards as a line of blood welled across my stomach.

X jerked his head back at the sight and dropped the knife. In the next second his hands were on me. "*Angel,*" he said, horrified, as though he hadn't meant to turn the weapon on me in the first place. He probably hadn't. Gambler must've compelled him to do so.

A steady stream of blood still trickled out of my wound. "It should've healed by now," I said, staring down at it. It continued to bleed.

X angled the cut towards himself to get a better look, and I honed in on the action. Most of his hand pressed against the fabric of my suit, but his thumb, his thumb touched bare skin.

"Holy shit," I breathed, as a thought hit me.

"What?" X's grip tightened.

"Let go of me."

Immediately he released me. As soon as he did so, the skin resumed healing. I watched it until the seam of skin sealed itself completely over, leaving behind only a mess of blood. Only then did I tear my eyes away to look at him.

"We really do cancel out each other's powers."

CHAPTER 21

"Tʜᴀᴛ'ꜱ ɴᴏᴛ ɢᴏᴏᴅ, Angel," I finally said, standing up.

In fact, it was very, very fucking bad, now that I'd had a change of plans.

I was supposed to leave her here. But now that the Cruel Countess knew our location, she could no longer stay.

The Gambler let out a small noise, reminding me that the fucker had burrowed into my mind and taken over.

No tolerance.

I turned on the Gambler.

Don't kill him. Not in front of Angel. She'll never forgive you.

I grabbed the Gambler. "Get. Out. Of. My. Fucking. Head," I said as his screams started up again.

Killing him took seconds. It should've taken longer.

Would've, if Angel hadn't stood at my back. He'd been right about that. I curbed my violence because of her.

I dropped him only once a blackened husk remained. As his body collapsed on the ground, flakes of ash drifted off of him.

Angel staggered back at the sight. "*Christ.*"

It didn't matter at this point if she loved me or hated me. Keeping her safe was my top priority, and it got just a little bit harder now that there was nowhere safe to leave her. If the Cruel Countess somehow figured out what we just did—that I could halt her rapid healing—she'd use me against Angel.

Another liability. One neither of us would survive.

I rubbed my lower lip. She had to come with me then. And then, when the time was right, I'd have to abandon her.

Angel

WHEN X TURNED the car into the marina, I glanced around. He'd kept ominously quiet, his knuckles white from gripping the wheel. I'd thought it wise to leave him be. The last person to piss him off ended up as a pile of ash.

But staring out at the open waters that would take me away from land, away from my sister—I was done with his mantrum.

"I'm not fleeing with you, X," I said, my hand going to the car handle. I'd jump out if it came to it.

Something fierce and possessive clouded his expression. "Let go of the door, Angel. We're not running."

"Then why are we here?" I asked, taking in the rows of moored boats.

"The Cruel Countess doesn't exactly live on land."

I could've used that piece of information a bit earlier. It made me wonder what else X had kept from me.

He'd been so gentle last night. I'd almost forgotten all that this man was capable of.

He killed for you, Angel. For your sister. And he was coming with me, heading towards what could surely be his death if all that he said about the Cruel Countess was true.

He's not just the cold-hearted brute I took him for, I thought as I watched him. My throat worked. It was so much easier when I thought of X as such. Then he'd been expendable. Now the thought of him going into the Cruel Countess's fortress did uncomfortable things to my stomach.

"So where does the Cruel Countess live?" I asked, returning my thoughts to the task at hand. "On the water?"

X shook his head. "Not on the water—beneath it."

The Executioner didn't just own expansive homes. He had at least one boat as well.

"This is yours?" I asked, staring down what looked like some combination of yacht and powerboat. It had a streamline design, a railed-in space to sit or lay along the bow, and a semi-enclosed cockpit and possibly an interior room below deck.

"Company boat," X explained, heading up the gangway

with our bags.

I spent the next ten minutes helping X unmoor the boat and watching him in front of the captain's chair as he powered it up. The navigation system was much more modernized than what I was used to, but the same concepts applied. Wheel, throttle, and levers and buttons for the anchor, lights, and so on.

As soon as we hit open ocean, he gunned the engine. We skipped over swells, and the wind whipped my hair behind me.

"Know how to use scuba gear?" he yelled over the sound of the engine.

Vaguely. I'd begun taking a class a couple years ago, but after garnering too many onlookers, the instructor quietly asked me to reschedule for private lessons. I never did.

"Yeah," I said. Not *wholly* a lie.

X stared at me long enough for me to think he didn't believe me, but eventually he nodded. "Gear's below deck."

I squinted. "How long will it take to get there?"

"Twelve hours, give or take."

"*Twelve hours?*" The clock in X's car had read that it was a little after one in the morning. That put our arrival sometime in the afternoon. "I thought you said it was just off the coast?"

"It is. The Caribbean is a large body of water."

Twelve hours. Twelve hours for the Cruel Countess to tear into my sister. Twelve hours to worry we wouldn't pull this off. Twelve hours to not give into my desire for this man.

I left the cockpit and headed for the bow, where the tip of the boat cut through water. Twelve hours.

And then we'd get my sister back.

AFTER ABOUT AN hour of driving, X came out from behind the helm with a beer in either hand. He found me on the deck, where I brooded, anxious.

"Pacifico?" X asked, holding out one of the drinks.

"Please," I said, taking it from him.

I took a swig of the beer while X sat down, leaning against the sloped windows of his boat.

"Don't you need to keep steering?" I asked.

"I set the navigation system to autopilot."

"Ah."

Setting his drink aside, X unzipped his jacket and shrugged it off. Then he grabbed the edges of his long-sleeved shirt and pulled it over his head.

I lowered the Pacifico from my face and watched him. Hard stomach muscles rippled.

Holy mother of ... that body just wasn't fair.

X caught me looking and he raised a brow.

"It's all so white—that's why I'm staring," I said, bringing the beer back to my lips.

I sat down next to him, despite my legs having the jitters.

"I hate this," I said, breathing in the briny smell of the sea.

"Mmm," he agreed, tilting his beer back and taking a swallow of it.

"How did you deal with the anger and fear when it was your brother she held against you?"

He glanced over at me before facing the water once more. "I made others feel my suffering and earned a name for my ruthlessness."

Yeah, that wasn't helpful advice.

I set my drink aside and stretched out on my back. Next to me, X followed suit, wrapping his forearm behind his head.

The stars twinkled above us, unbelievably bright now that we were on open water.

"Will I die tomorrow?" I asked.

"No." He said the word with such determination, like he alone would make sure of exactly that. Odd to have a supervillain trying to save your life.

"Will you die tomorrow?"

"No," he said, his voice less sure.

I rolled my head to the side to face him. My eyes traced his features. The way moonlight made his eyes glint, the shadows that threw his cheekbones into sharp relief. Those lips ...

He glanced over at me. "What?"

"You're still willing to face the Cruel Countess even though you might die?"

His brow furrowed. "Yes."

One of the wickedest villains in the world was going to put his life on the line for my sister. It didn't matter what his motives were, he was willing to die for me.

I reached over and traced the veins of his hand with my fingers. X closed his eyes, savoring the feel of it. This man who'd been denied so much, who'd suffered so much, and who'd used his terrible power for good before the Cruel Countess recruited him. He'd let everyone think him soulless, even himself.

But he wasn't.

I turned the rest of my body on its side to face him. He gave me a sidelong look, a small frown on his face.

"Wh—"

I leaned forward and pressed a kiss to his lips, his warm, soft lips. My hand drifted up, rubbing the stubble along his cheek, then delved into his hair.

Earlier he'd turned me down, and he might again. I was willing to chance my feelings.

For a moment, he did nothing, and I thought that whatever had stopped him earlier would stop him again. But a second later, he reacted, his lips moving against mine.

He began slow, tentative, savoring the glide of our lips. Kisses like this one moved you, made you believe in things like soul mates and true love.

He broke away, angling his body so that he was now on his side, staring back at me.

"Don't stop," I pleaded.

A ghost of a smile touched his lips, and then he was back to kissing me, his breath hot.

His arm snaked around my waist and drew me in until I was pressed against those hard abs of his.

Fucking villains and their perfect bodies ...

X parted my lips with his own, and then his tongue stroked mine. My mouth caught his groan. Our lips moved together, faster, more frantic, and this time I broke away, reaching for his hand. Once I grasped it, I guided it to my suit's zipper.

His eyes widened for the briefest of seconds—like I'd asked him to dismantle a bomb—before he focused on drawing the zipper down.

Material peeled away, and he stared at what he saw.

"Take it off me," I said.

He hesitated. "Are you ... sure?" his gravelly voice was a whisper on the breeze.

"You might be the first supervillain in history to ask that question," I teased. "Of course I'm sure."

X's gaze burned through me as he resumed his work. He pushed the material over one shoulder, and then the other, entranced by the sight of my skin. His hands glided over it, and his eyes, his eyes ...

He leaned in, towards the hollow of my throat and pressed the barest of kisses there. As he did so, he slid the rest of the top off my arms, exposing my torso.

He exhaled sharply. Ever so gently, he guided me so that my back lay against the floor. He came with me.

His mouth found mine again, and as he kissed me before his hands returned to the suit.

He dragged it off agonizingly slow, transfixed by every new inch of skin it uncovered, until it was completely gone.

This must be new for him. Had he ever reveled over another's body the way he was mine? So much had been denied to this man.

But it would be denied no longer.

I let him soak up the moment, not hurrying him, not

trying to rip his own pants off, until finally, I couldn't wait any longer.

I sat up and began unbuttoning his jeans, brushing him in the process. He groaned and took over for me, removing the rest of his clothes in record time.

All that was left were my itsy bitsy panties, and he knelt, removing those too before settling himself over me.

Now we stared into each other's eyes. Looking into his, I realized that I didn't see the Executioner, I saw a handsome, broken man who, beneath all that dangerous skin, desperately wanted to redeem himself. I saw Sam.

X pressed into me and I arched my pelvis up, meeting him as he glided into me. He stared down at me all the while, watching my eyes flutter and the sigh roll out of me.

Thunderstruck. That was his expression as he thrust into me, gripping my thigh and angling me to get as close as possible.

He watched my reaction, perhaps disbelieving that he could possibly be giving me pleasure. "Does that … ?"

"Feels amazing," I breathed, staring up at him. He rocked into me again and I moaned. "Harder."

His body shivered as he met my demand.

Euphoria. Rapture. That was what it felt like to be in this man's arms. By the time I came apart around him and he collapsed on top of me, something in his eyes had changed. There was a new spark there. Hope alighted in his eyes, but so did something else, something that had my stomach clench with excitement even as dread bathed my body.

The Executioner feels something for me.

Cupping my cheeks, he kissed me fiercely. X tasted warm and rich against my chilly face. I pinched my eyes shut as I kissed him back.

Something a lot like happiness pooled low in my belly.

Please not now, and not with him. My stupid body couldn't be reasoned with.

I'd stayed away from relationships for this very reason. For someone like me, being with another was a sticky business, one that promised a future of pain. In my line of work, civilians were used as leverage, heroes could be killed, and loved ones were exploited. Our situation was proof of that.

But heaven help me, X might not be the only one developing feelings.

CHAPTER 22

Executioner

THE QUIET BEEP of my watch's alarm roused me from sleep. I woke with a tangle of caramel hair splayed across my chest and a beautiful woman draped across my side.

I am the luckiest son of a gun out there.

If I thought that sex would kick the urge to be with Angel, I thought *wrong*.

I turned off my alarm and got up, glancing down at Angel as I did so. Something in my chest tightened at the sight of her. *Mine.* The word wrapped itself around me. We might be a long ways off from love, but tonight felt like the first of many to come.

I couldn't let her go. I wouldn't. Right then and there I decided it. If she wanted me to hang up my career—which she would, because a woman like that wouldn't just settle for a thug—then I would. I'd even atone. And I'd make damn sure that come tomorrow, I would find her sister and get us out of there alive.

Because now I truly had something to live for.

She moaned as I slid out from under her.

That sound! Never would it get old.

"Where are you going?" she asked.

"I'm checking the navigation system and grabbing us some blankets."

I slipped away and grabbed the pile of linens stashed below the helm and brought them back to Angel. Shaking them out, I laid one after another over her, hoping upon hope that this would keep her warm enough to continue sleeping long after I disappeared.

Her lips curled up. Content. I'd made this woman content—if only for a short while. A pang of regret slammed into my chest. If only ...

Before I could do something idiotic like rejoin her, I backed away and headed to the boat's cockpit to check over the measures I put in place earlier. The satellite phone was fully charged, the autopilot nav system was up and running, the lies had been seeded.

Time to go.

I'd misled Angel earlier. It wouldn't take us half a day to get to the Cruel Countess's lair. Only a handful of hours.

I'd purposefully set the boat's course to overshoot the Cruel Countess's lair before turning around and cutting back across it. I would disembark there, while the powerboat would continue on until it hit the mainland. So long as nothing cataclysmic happened to the boat, Angel should wake up beached on the sand.

Better odds than if she came with me.

As quietly as I could, I worked the wetsuit over my skin and slid on my scuba gear. All set.

My eyes drifted back to her. She quietly snored underneath the stars.

Goddamn that woman.

Life had never been fair or easy, and now was no exception. I should be there next to her, claiming sleep like I owned it, and not sneaking away on a suicide mission.

It's not too late! I could chart a new course and drag Angel kicking and screaming away from this place. Leave her sister here to die. Wouldn't be the worst crime I'd ever committed.

But something had taken root, something—I cringed to admit—halfway decent.

I pulled on the last of my gear, checked the buoyancy compensator, the weights, the releases, and the tank's pressure. All good. Nothing to keep me here any longer.

One last look.

Her brows furrowed in her sleep, like she sensed that I was about to deceive her. It was a physical thing, stopping myself from going to her and smoothing out those brows.

Can't do that.

Even now she could wake up and derail the entire plan.

I moved to the edge of the boat, pulled down my face-mask and fitted the mouthpiece. I watched the navigation readout, waiting until we were directly overhead the Cruel Countess's compound.

Sleep well, Angel.

I slid into the water as quietly as I could and began my descent.

It felt like someone had chained and padlocked my lungs, seeing the powerboat motor on, carrying my super-hero away from me.

Survive, and you'll see her again.

I dove, moving farther and farther away from the water's surface, pausing only for my body to adjust to the pressure.

By the time I saw the first pinpricks of light beneath me, I was positive the Cruel Countess knew I'd come.

Her beloved sharks circled me, swimming with agitated flicks of their tails. Urban legend said that the first power the Countess had ever stolen was the ability to speak to animals. I'd never seen her exert this power firsthand, but I knew she wielded it. The few times I'd entered the Cruel Countess's lair this way, her sharks were always careful never to touch me—I was sure she instructed them not to bite. Not for my sake, of course. That, she'd enjoy. No, she worried her little *beasties* would perish.

God, I hated that broad.

There would be no escape for me unless I killed the Cruel Countess. I also knew my chances of ending her were slim.

The lights beneath me brightened as I got closer, shining along the contours of the underwater compound. Through some of the building's thick windows I could see in. The place looked abandoned.

Lights on but nobody home.

I moved around the compound to the underwater cave that led to the building's back door. I entered, and lights strung up along the cavern's ceiling shone far above me, illuminating the space in blues and greens.

The sharks that circled me now tightened their formation. I kicked out, nicking one of their noses with my fin. With an agitated twist, the shark withdrew from my side.

Screw what Angel said, fish were *most definitely* food.

The surface of the water rippled above me. I broke through it and pushed myself out to a rocky outcropping.

I took my time removing the wetsuit, knowing full that the Cruel Countess waited for me.

She could wait a little longer.

I stripped down to my boxer briefs and, grabbing my gear, headed to the end of the cave, where an armored door was embedded into the cavernous wall.

The door swung open before I had a chance to enter the Cruel Countess's code into the keypad. I entered the white hallway, feeling the pressure of being so far below the sea. No one milled around. There should've been guards and supervillains roaming this place.

I headed over to the row of lockers and, when I found mine, I tossed my gear inside and grabbed the spare suit I'd left folded on the top shelf.

"You were supposed to bring me the girl."

I rotated away from the locker. The Cruel Countess stood there, looking like a twenty-five year old vixen. In reality she was over three times that age. Just another power she'd siphoned away, this one to fuel her vanity.

"And yet I didn't," I said, dropping my boxer briefs and

pulling on my fresh clothes.

She blatantly eyed me, hungry for what she couldn't have. Envy ruled the Cruel Countess, and because she wouldn't risk touching me and hurting herself, she could never own my power. And that, in turn, made her want me all the more.

Her shoes clicked on the linoleum floor, her crimson dress dragging behind her. "You. Defied. Me."

I pulled my leather jacket on over my shirt, leaving the hood down. "I need Angel's sister."

She raised her eyebrows, an amused smile blooming on her face. "Oh you do now?" She was legitimately curious. And that was the other thing about the Cruel Countess. The unexpected delighted her—intrigued her—even when it pissed her off. "But I thought you didn't care whether she lived or died."

"I don't." I did. "Give her to me in whatever state you'd like."

She tapped a finger to her cheek. "Hmmm ..." She eyed me for several seconds before snapping her fingers. In the next instant, several of her guards appeared at her side. I knew they didn't have the ability to teleport, which meant she'd cloaked them. Sneaky.

"Thrall," she said to one of the female guards at her side, "tell me what the Executioner is hiding."

Thrall, the stealer of thoughts. She stared hard at me. I tried to block the intrusion, tried to seal my secrets from her, but it was pointless. I could feel her rifling through my thoughts, as memory after unbidden memory flittered through my mind.

"He can touch the healer without killing her," Thrall said.

The Cruel Countess raised an eyebrow, appraising him once more. "Interesting."

"Their powers cancel out. When they touch, he can't hurt her, she can't heal him, and she cannot heal herself."

"*Very* interesting." I could feel the Countess's anger licking along my skin, yet she remained playful.

"She's on a boat heading for Miami," Thrall said.

The Cruel Countess's lips made a moue. "Miami? You brought her all this way only to keep her from me?" She clucked her tongue. "That will cost you, Executioner."

My jaw clenched.

Her eyes roved over me again. "Once I have her power, I'll no longer have to hold back touching you."

I suppressed a shudder. Few people frightened me. She was one of them.

"More," the Cruel Countess demanded.

"They've fucked," Thrall said.

The Cruel Countess's eyes widened, her mouth forming an O. "Really now? Did you drug her, X, or simply force her while she was awake?"

My hands fisted.

"Consensual," Thrall supplied.

The Countess's face hardened. "Thrall, get Tracker and find the girl."

I had to school my features to stop myself from reacting.

Angel, you better be one fucking competent superhero.

Thrall broke away from the group, her boots echoed on the tiled floor as she left the hall.

"You defied me," the Cruel Countess said. "Not once, but over and over again."

I leaned against the locker next to mine and folded my arms. "I did," I agreed.

She raised her arm and flicked her wrist. The motion lifted me off my feet and propelled me across the hallway. I slammed into the lockers bolted to the other wall. They buckled beneath me, their metal handles digging into my side.

Another flick of her wrist and I was dragged back to her, my feet never touching the ground.

"You thought you could steal the healer from me?" The walls hummed as her power vibrated through them. Water began dripping from the corners of the ceiling, and rivulets of it snaked down the walls.

"*Answer me!*" she screamed, compulsion riding her voice.

"*Yes.*" The answer ripped through me.

Water continued to drip down the walls, pooling around the Cruel Countess.

"*How dare you!*" Phantom fingers dug into my skin, slicing the flesh in a hundred different locations. Pain bloomed across my body.

The Cruel Countess brought me right up to her face. "I could snap your neck right now."

I could feel it, the pressure constricting my windpipe, tugging my head to the side.

"I could drown you this very instant." At her words the water at the Countess's feet slithered over to me. It crawled up my legs, dampening, then drying my pants as

154

it moved higher and higher.

I stared at the Countess, refusing to fight this, to show any reaction at all, even as the water snaked in through my nostrils and into my mouth. I began to choke as it dripped down my lungs.

The Countess watched me, her anger abating as I struggled to breathe.

"I could end you so quickly." The water retreated from my lungs. "But you deserve worse." Water and blood from my cuts dripped from my toes, puddling on the ground beneath me.

She turned on her heal. "Come."

With a yank, my body was dragged forward once more.

"How desperate must you be to come into my territory," she mused. "Let me guess, Angel wanted you to retrieve her sister."

Another yank and I floated at her side. *No better than a fucking marionette.*

"What a terrible, terrible situation. The first girl you can touch without hurting is going to die. And I'm going to make you watch."

CHAPTER 23

Angel

I STRETCHED OUT, my limbs shaking as I did so. A smile tugged at the edges of my lips.

Shouldn't feel this happy. My sister is missing. The thought had my eyes snapping open.

I heard the cry of a gull above me.

A bird? But we're out in open water ...

I sat up, rubbing my eyes, gathering the blankets to my chest. Blankets X had covered me with last night. Another grin slipped out.

"X?" I called.

No answer.

I turned to the cockpit. No one manned it.

Perhaps he's below deck.

"X?" I said again.

The smile slipped.

I grabbed my suit and yanked it on. Something wasn't right.

Had he returned to bed? I couldn't be sure.

I headed over to the helm and paused when I caught sight of the screen's readout.

"No ..."

I glanced up, and sure enough, in the distance I could make out Miami.

My gaze returned to the mapped route, which cut across some mystery point X had inputted—likely the Cruel Countess's lair—and continued on, leading back to the mainland. I stared at the screen for a long moment.

I didn't know how I was supposed to feel. Anger—yes plenty of that. That bastard betrayed me. Confusion, because why? Why would he leave me to go alone?

Then fear, so much fear, rose to the back of my throat. *What will happen to my sister? What will happen to X?*

My jaw clenched. Nothing. Nothing would happen to them so long as I drew in air.

I sat down in the captain's chair. I grew up in San Diego, and my father loved to take me fishing near the Coronado islands. I'd had enough exposure to his boat to get how they worked. This one wasn't too different.

Did X really think that I wouldn't be able to override his flimsy plan?

I reversed the GPS, redirecting the boat to its source. Quickly, I moved throughout the boat, taking inventory of the stacked gallons of gasoline. Heading back to the wheel, I checked the fuel remaining in the engine. The readout told me 23 percent remained.

Not much.

Perhaps not even enough to get back to the mainland, depending on wind resistance and the choppiness of the ocean. I turned the boat around and redirected my course to that speck out in open water.

I caught sight of X's cooler and the bottle opener lying next to it. Leaning down, I grabbed a Pacifico from the ice chest and popped it open. The sky lightened to the east.

I took a swig of beer, then pushed the throttle forward.

Fuck it, today was a decent enough day to die.

I FLIPPED ON the boat's sound system, then grabbed my cell, which I'd haphazardly tossed onto one of the seats.

Thank God for satellite phones. I flipped through the caller ID until I stopped on a cartoon drawing of Lewis Carroll's Mad Hatter. Before I had a chance to hit *Send*, my phone began to ring, and the Mad Hatter's crazy face took up the screen.

"Hey Madman," I answered.

"You're going to die today."

I pulled the phone away from my ear, stared at it, then cradled it against my head once more. "You could've eased me into that one a little more gently."

"Honesty is the best policy."

"Ah, but the future changes."

"That it does," he agreed.

I squinted out at the sea. "How would you like to bring

down the Cruel Countess?"

"Angel, I am literally thirty-five steps ahead of you—oh, don't shoot Dolly Parton."

"What?" Holding a conversation with the Madman often made me feel insane. I could only imagine what it was like to live in his head. "Hey, by the way, is Marc still safe?" I asked.

"Marc sucks at *Halo*. Bring a better hostage next time."

I ducked into the small stateroom beneath the deck, looking for scuba gear. No such luck. The bastard never had a second dive suit. "Marc's not a hostage. Is he safe?"

"Define 'safe.'"

I groaned. I was going to be in deep if X saved my sister only to find out that something happened to Marc.

"The gun is under one of the seats behind the captain's chair."

"What gun?"

"The one you'll try to shoot Dolly with."

I eyed the semicircle of seats Madman spoke of. Hmmm.

"The day toils on. Much ado, so little time. Get ready to rock."

"Right on, Maddy Baddy." I clicked the phone off. On the horizon, I noticed a blip. A boat?

I grabbed binoculars from one of the cockpit's nearby compartments and peered through them. Definitely a boat, and it was coming straight for me.

That can't be good.

I moved towards the seats Madman spoke of. Grasping the soft vinyl seat bottom, I lifted up.

"Ho-ly Fukushima." There wasn't just a gun, there was

a whole stash of them. *And a rocket launcher.* A loaded one.

"Supervillains ..." I muttered.

I grabbed an M16 fitted with a scope and idled the engine.

Bracing the assault rifle between my arms, I leaned over the seatbacks and watched the boat approach through the weapon's lens. It could just be a fishing boat, or someone taking their yacht out for a spin. I hoped it was.

But I doubted it.

Just to be safe, I checked the magazine. Fully loaded.

I shook my head. "Villains."

I didn't have to lay in wait long. The boat hopped over waves, its bow bobbing in the water. I watched the riders in my scope. I could see three of them, all dressed in black fatigues and wearing the symbol of the Cruel Countess—a crest with two interlocked C's held up by two dragons.

How did they know where to find me?

I lined up the sights and fired a warning shot.

The three ducked, then immediately reached for the weapons holstered around their waists.

X must've gotten caught. That or he betrayed me.

I thought over the last few days. He could keep his emotions on lock down, but I could read the naked want on his face. The idea of being able to touch another without hurting them was stronger than any forced alliance.

So, not betrayal then.

A shot pinged against the side of the boat.

I drew in a steadying breath. Lining up the sights once more, I aimed, then fired. One of the three went down. The other two gaped at their fallen comrade. While they did so, I fired again.

The third dropped to one knee, and a shot rang out. A split second later, the bullet embedded itself into my shoulder.

Mother of God. I collapsed onto the seat and clutched the wound. It had torn through the muscle of my rotator cuff. I knew as soon as my wound screamed anew that the bullet hadn't exited my body. Yet.

I gritted my teeth as the metal worked its way back through its entry point, scraping against bone as it dislodged itself.

I so needed another beer for this.

Another shot pinged against the side of the boat. The bastards were trying to sink me. They shot me and now they wanted to sink me. My famous anger welled up.

I lifted the vinyl seats once more, ignoring the blood that dripped from my wound into the compartment. As I stared at the guns, my shoulder purged the bullet, and it clinked right next to the weapon I was looking for.

"Hello lovely," I said, grabbing the rocket launcher.

They just pissed off the wrong woman.

I propped the weapon up. I'd only ever used one of these once, and that ended with an exploded camper and seven angry superheroes. *Here's to hoping this turns out better.*

Ping, ping, ping. Bullets embedded themselves into the starboard side. The shooter must've caught sight of the rocket launcher since the firing sounded more frequent and frantic. I ignored him, lining up the sights and moving my aim to the back of the Cruel Countess's boat, where the engine rested.

"*Sayonara, assholes.*" I pulled the trigger.

The kickback nearly threw me to the ground. The missile hissed across the waves, then—

BOOM.

The boat blew apart, shooting bits of fiberglass, people, and wooden beams into the air. The force of it sent a huge wave rocking against the boat, and I grabbed the seat for stability.

Within seconds the entire thing was over. The enemy boat smoldered, its remains swallowed by water.

I set the rocket launcher back into the compartment, then headed for the wheel, stretching out my previously injured shoulder. I cranked up the throttle and the music and resumed course, leaving behind all evidence of my anger.

And that was why people didn't piss me off. Because angels, sweet as we are, do from time to time ...

Fall.

CHAPTER 24

Angel

I'D ONLY RESUMED course for five minutes when another boat popped up on the horizon.

I lowered my binoculars. "You've got to be kidding me." It was like disturbing a beehive—once you pissed a few of them off, the rest were quick to avenge the slight.

"It was just one boat." And three supervillains, but what are details?

I grabbed the M16 once more, watching this new boat approach.

As they got closer, I lined up my sights and fired a warning shot. The boat didn't slow.

I got ready to fire again when it began to turn, giving me its starboard side. I squinted, my eyes passing over the vessel. My trigger finger froze as I caught sight of the boat's name.

Dolly Parton.

I let out a shaky breath and set the gun aside. *Don't shoot Dolly Parton.* That was what Madman had been referring to. A boat.

I ran my hands through my hair, shaken by how close I'd come to shooting my friends.

I idled the engine and waved my hands in the air. *Dolly Parton* circled me. When I didn't shoot again, she closed in. I first caught sight of Zeus, his signature thunderbolt clutched tightly in his hand.

Rocket lifted off the boat, flying over to me. I smiled up at him as he descended, landing several feet in front of me. "Seems like you're a magnet for trouble these days," he said. His eyes scanned the boat, pausing on the weapons.

I huffed out a laugh. "You have no idea."

Rocket flew us to the *Dolly Parton.*

"This time you only shot at us once. An improvement," Madman said when we landed.

I stepped out of Rocket's arms. "What's going on?"

I hadn't realized that when I'd called Madman, he'd already been on this side of the country. I took in the group—Rocket, Zeus, Zephyr, Cinder—short for Incindiary, the pyrotechnic of the group—and ...

"Chameleon?"

My friends had the guy tied up. "This one tried to kidnap Marc," Aries said, patting Chameleon on the shoulder. The man winced. "But it looks like the kidnapper got kidnapped."

Cinder approached the supervillain, her hips swaying in her red suit. She had that whole Jessica Rabbit thing working for her—great curves, sexy red hair, and sensual features. She was also one of L.A.S.D.'s deadliest superheroes, if the explosives that circled her waist were any indication. Her being here indicated that whatever happened today, it would be big.

Cinder caressed Chameleon's cheek. "We were just in the middle of discussing the location of Cruel Countess's lair."

Chameleon eyed Cinder's hands, and I could see the whites of his own. I guess she'd already had fun with him.

"He's going to lie, then get us all killed," Madman said before Chameleon had a chance to reply.

"N-no, I'm not."

"Lie," Madman said.

Zeus held a thunderbolt in his hand. "Easy way or hard way, Chameleon, it's your choice."

Cinder snapped her thumb and forefinger, and five small flames blossomed on her fingertips. "Either way, we'll get what we want," she said leaning in until her flames licked his face.

Chameleon screamed as the fire burned his cheek. "I'll talk, I'll talk!"

Cinder drew her hand away, but didn't extinguish the flames.

As Chameleon began to mutter an answer, Madman

left the group, heading back for the captain's chair. I followed him.

He began to navigate the boat, his eyes unfocused. I'd seen him this way before, knew what it meant.

"Tell him that castration comes next!" Madman suddenly shouted to Zeus and Cinder, earning a head nod from the former and a wicked smile from the latter. Madman whistled. "*Now* we're in business."

I placed my hand over Madman's, trying to heal his addled mind. I felt him shudder under my touch.

"Thanks," he said, his eyes still unfocused.

"I should be saying that to you. Why did you all come?"

"To help you take out the Cruel Countess. You couldn't do it without us."

My lips parted. "You ... saw me die?" It was odd to think that a version of me had already gone after my sister—gone after her and failed.

Madman nodded. "Now we'll all just probably die. Much better odds."

"You all came to help me." I couldn't quite catch my breath. I'd always thought of my teammates as friends, but never had they proven their friendship like this.

He smiled. "Always, Angel."

It took twenty minutes and some back and forth between X's boat and *Dolly*, but eventually we found the Cruel Countess's lair. I'd taken over steering while Madman sat in one of the boat's seats, clutching his head.

"Now what?" Rocket asked.

"... knows we're here knows we're here knows we're here," Madman mumbled.

His head snapped up. "Moses." His eyes searched the deck, alighting on Zephyr. He nodded. "Moses."

I raised an eyebrow, not sure where he was going with this. And then it clicked. "Zephyr!" I waved her over.

"What's up?" she said, coming to the back of the boat.

"Madman wants you to part the sea." If we could get past the water, we could have free access to the Cruel Countess's fortress.

Zephyr's eyes widened and looked over at Madman. He was moaning, clutching his head. "I don't know if I have that kind of power."

"Twice." Madman lowered his hands. "In and out. In and out. In and—"

Now it was Zephyr's turn to rub her head. "You want me to do this twice? This is going to kill me."

"Maybe, six fifty-two. You die, she dies, we all die some of the time."

I headed over to Madman and touched his hand again. He drew in a ragged breath. "I need a drink," he said, lucid once more.

I squeezed his hand. "If we make it out of this alive, margaritas are on me."

Madman's eyes focused on mine. "The Cruel Countess knows we're here. She wants you, Angel, and only you can take her out. We might survive, but she has a telepathist as well. It's a mental chess battle."

I frowned.

His gaze moved to Zephyr. "Six thirteen. Aim true. You

may have your doubts, but you'll know what to do."

"Aim?" she said.

I checked my phone.

6:10 a.m.

I stuck two fingers in my mouth and whistled loudly. Rocket, Cinder, and Zeus paused their interrogation to glance over.

"Listen up guys: this water is going to part in three minutes. We should be directly over the Cruel Countess's lair. Get ready. We're about to go in!"

Whoops came from the other side of the boat. I checked my weapons while Zephyr's eyes closed and her breaths evened out.

The ocean rippled, as though a large, invisible stone had been skipped along it.

Madman moaned from his seat. "In and out, in and out—a cave." He began laughing. "A *cave*."

"We're going to get you those margaritas real soon, Madman," I promised.

Sea spray sprinkled over my skin, bringing my attention back to the ocean. Zephyr's wind carved into the water, making a donut around the boat. She stretched her hands in front of her.

Zeus, Cinder, and Rocket came to the back of the boat. Chameleon remained secured at the front, his hair clearly singed.

I furrowed my brows. "Who hogtied the supervillain?" I asked.

Zeus looked him over. "I didn't go to cowboy camp for nothing."

My hair whipped about as Zephyr's wind hit us and the boat dipped. I grabbed the handrail. A shadow passed over us, causing me to glance up.

Holy shit.

A column of water twenty feet high encircled us, and it kept rising. I stared up at it as it twisted around us. Next to me Zephyr's outstretched hands shook and her eyes fluttered.

The light dimmed the farther we descended, and the water darkened. Next to me, the ends of Cinder's hair caught fire, casting some dim light on the boat. Shadows danced around us, a strange play of firelight and water.

I caught her eye and she winked, flashing me a sultry smile. "Heard about you and the Executioner," she said. "Supervillains are fun, aren't they?"

I licked my dry lips, not sure how to respond to that.

She laughed at my expression.

Our conversation was—thankfully—interrupted as the boat hit the ocean floor.

"Now what?" Rocket asked, looking around at our barren surroundings.

I hopped over the edge and into ankle-deep water. "Now we move."

"Hate to break it to you Zephyr," Rocket said, "but I think you dropped us into the wrong location."

If Zephyr had indeed lowered us anywhere but on top of the Cruel Countess's lair, then we'd have to surface and try again.

The others hopped off alongside me. The rocky surface beneath my feet seemed like a far cry from the white sand I'd imagined.

"Cave," Madman reminded us.

Cave … ? I didn't see any gaping entrances.

"Guys," I could barely hear Zephyr's shout over the roar of the water, "I can't hold this for much longer." As if to prove her point, the churning column of water wavered, then tightened in on us. "I'm going to have to bring the boat back up."

"We're looking!" Cinder shouted, pissy because seawater kept snuffing out her flaming locks, "but it's really fucking dark, and your aim might've been shit."

I rounded the boat. Here the ground dipped. I nearly slipped when the ground dropped off and the water deepened. I toed the edge.

An underwater cave entrance? It sounded absurd, even in my head.

I glanced over at Madman, who was still onboard. His lost gaze found mine and he gave me two thumbs up.

Good enough for me.

I whistled again. "Over here!" I shouted. I lowered myself to the ledge, my legs swallowed up by the water. The cyclone circling us twisted tighter and tighter.

"Guys!" Zephyr yelled.

My teammates—all save for Madman and Zephyr—rounded the boat, splashing water with them. The three of them seemed particularly miffed about being surrounded by so much water. Little wonder—this much liquid could cripple flight, snuff out flame, and overpower electricity.

I heard Zephyr's scream over the wind.

Uh oh.

"Hurry!" I shouted as the water I sat in rose to my chest.

They closed the distance between us, Cinder slipping as she overshot the lip I sat on.

"I think the cave's beneath us," I said.

"You *think?*" Rocket yelled. "You mean this is just a guess?"

"We're going to have to dive under!" I shouted over him to the others.

I heard Cinder swear under her breath. The others nodded.

The water continued to rise as the wind died.

"Dive!" I ducked under the water, shoving my body under the lip I sat on.

Please be the cave. Please don't drown.

I desperately hoped I read Madman correctly. Otherwise I'd sentenced the four of us to our deaths.

Behind me, a light flickered on. I glanced back to see a glowing Zeus, flanked by Rocket and Cinder. He used his electricity to glow in the dark. The light illuminated the contours of the cave. When I faced forward again, I could see the water's surface. I swam to it.

Six fifty-two.

6:52

That was what Madman said. Zephyr would come for us again.

My head broke the surface, and I drew in a lungful of air. Three other heads came up behind me.

I caught sight of a rocky outcropping on one side of the

cave, and beyond it, a door bolted into the wall. We swam to it, hefting ourselves out of the water.

"Ugh, I hate getting wet," Cinder said. Her body went up in flame. When she finally put it out, she was completely dry. Her flame-retardant suit managed to stay pristine through it all.

"Well, there went my gun," Rocket said, pulling out the dripping metal he'd tucked into his suit.

Cinder leaned over and blew flame over the gun.

Rocket yelped and dropped the weapon. "Seriously, Cinder?" he said as I touched him, healing whatever trace burns she might've given him.

She rolled her eyes and picked up the gun. "Stop being a baby." Her flame encircled the gun, evaporating the last of the water. "All better," she said, handing it back.

Ignoring their bickering, I headed to the door.

Less than an hour. That was all the time I had to find X and my sister and save them.

When I reached the door, I tried the handle. It swung open.

What were the odds of that?

I glanced behind me, where Cinder was still squabbling with Rocket and Zeus.

Get your sister. Get X. The need pulsed through my veins.

I stepped inside. As soon as I'd crossed the threshold, the door slammed shut.

"What a pleasant surprise, Angel." The Cruel Countess's voice rang out. "You're exactly the girl I wanted to see."

Aw fuck, another trap.

CHAPTER 25

Angel

I GLANCED AROUND the empty hallway, looking for the Cruel Countess, but the place was abandoned.

"Come find me, Angel. A sibling reunion is in order."

I closed my eyes and swallowed. *This monster has my sister.*

Behind me I could hear dull banging as my teammates pounded on the door. I tried the handle, but it wouldn't budge.

I stepped away and moved down the hall. Lockers lined either side—several smashed inward. One hung open, and scuba gear rested inside. I headed over to it and touched the oxygen tank.

X had been here.

My gaze swept the room, taking in the dented lockers, the puddle in the center of the hallway, and the bloody drops of water that trailed out of the room. I'd seen enough crime scenes to know X had been ambushed.

I stepped away from the locker and followed the bloody trail down the corridor. It hooked right, and I stepped into another hallway, where the droplets continued on.

This was one of the most macabre crumb trails I'd ever followed.

I passed into a lab full of fancy medical equipment and messy readouts. Strange, sharp implements rested on trays, several of them caked with fresh blood. Caught in the liquid were several strands of platinum blonde hair.

Ashley's hair.

I fisted my hands. I knew what this was—scare tactics. But the Cruel Countess had misjudged me. This didn't frighten me. It didn't make me desperate. It made me angry. Violence towards innocents was another one of my buttons, and the Cruel Countess just pushed it.

I strode through the next open door with more resolve. The Cruel Countess was going down.

THE LAB GAVE way to yet another corridor, this one fitted with several iron doors.

The prison block.

A viewing window had been set into each door, and I peered through the first one. Inside, a huge, muscular man cradled his arm, which ended in a bloody stump. Sweat dripped from what I could see of his face. The wound had to be infected.

I tried the door handle. Locked.

The man glanced up, and I recoiled from the window. The side of his face was a mass of blisters and scars, and where he should've had an eye, he now only had an empty socket.

I peeked into the next door. Inside an emaciated woman rocked herself back and forth. Deep cuts criss-crossed her skin.

Who were these people? Superheroes? Loved ones?

No guards—or any other souls for that matter—watched the prisoners.

I moved from cell to cell, each one locked, and each one housing a wounded prisoner. I held my breath before looking through each new window, readying myself for the moment I'd catch sight of my sister's startling blonde hair or X's brooding stare.

I came to the end of the hallway. Neither was here.

Far behind me, I heard a dull thump and the ground trembled. Then a much louder boom. I braced myself against the wall as the building shook again. My teammates were making short work of that door.

I hesitated before I left the prison block, glancing back over the line of cells. According to Madman, we had less than an hour before we had to leave this place. An impossibly short amount of time. Regardless, I wouldn't leave these men and women behind. We'd either all make it, or I'd die trying.

"I'll be back for you," I said to the room, uncaring whether or not the prisoners could hear me, before I resumed my search.

On the other side of the row of cells, a hallway ended in a columned, open space. Several doors lined the inside wall across from me, one which was propped open.

"Countess, I'm getting bored," I said.

Laughter trickled in from the other side of the door. "You won't be in a minute." I could hear the promise in her voice.

I followed the bloody trail through the door and into an auditorium. Rows and rows of long, curved tables wrapped around the room, descending down to a central stage. Behind the stage was an entire wall of glass and, beyond it, the dark ocean.

The room was entirely devoid of human life, yet my skin prickled. Unseen eyes watched me. I could feel myself moving deeper into some trap the Cruel Countess had set, but what choice did I have?

Someone had propped open the door to the left of the stage, but the drops of blood never made it that far. Instead, they pooled on the center of the platform.

Drip ... drip.

I descended the stairs and stepped onto the stage.

"Just the woman we've been waiting for," the Cruel Countess's voice rang out. In the next instant, she appeared in front of me.

I staggered back, surprised. Her eyes flicked behind me, and I glanced over my shoulder.

Where before the rows and rows of seats were empty, now supervillains and regular criminals filled them. Some wore their iconic outfits, others sported guard uniforms, the Cruel Countess's emblem embossed onto their breast pocket.

"How ... ?"

"Mirage isn't the only woman known for her illusions."

My shoulders tensed as I faced the Countess once more.

"So happy you ... dropped by," she said. "That was quite an entrance you and your friends made. Too bad you were separated." She made a moue of disappointment.

I could practically hear the seconds, minutes ticking by. The Countess would waste them all chatting with me.

"Where's my sister?"

"So you're ready to talk business." Her heels clicked as she sauntered towards me, her absurd gown dragging behind her. "To answer your question, your sister is here with me—as is one of my disloyal employees." Her eyes flashed to the crowd of onlookers—a warning to those who thought to cross her.

The Cruel Countess lifted her hand, and Ashley and X appeared on either side of her. They floated in midair, both struggling to open their mouths and pull their arms away from where they were bound behind them.

I took an involuntary step forward. Tears streamed down Ashley's cheeks. An entire half of her face was swollen and bruised, and her blonde hair was matted to her brow and temples. Bruises stained the exposed skin of her arms.

I fisted my hands as my jaw tightened, fury rising at her battered state.

On the other side of the Cruel Countess, X struggled with angry jerks of his body to disentangle himself from the Countess's hold. Open wounds criss-crossed his body, as though someone spent hours slicing him up with a knife.

Drip ... ... drip ... ... drip ... ...

Drops of blood sluggishly fell from his feet to the ground. A sheen of sweat beaded along his brow, and his agonized eyes begged me to leave. He'd tried to get me away from this place, tried to save me from the horror of it, but damn it, I was a superhero, not a princess to lock away in a tower.

My eyes finally settled back on the Cruel Countess, and a corner of her mouth lifted in some sinister parody of a smirk.

"I was just getting started on these two," she said, reaching out. Ashley's body lowered, and the Cruel Countess stroked her cheek. My sister shut her eyes, her body trembling. It was all I could do not to lunge for the Countess and wrap my arms around her neck. But if I did that, I'd have dozens of villains on me in an instant.

"You've seen some of my more involved work," she said. A flick of her eyes to the back of the auditorium. To the cells of prisoners.

The Cruel Countess began to pace, clasping her hands behind her back. As she did so, she dragged Ashley and X along with her.

"The way I see it," the Cruel Countess said, turning on her heel. X and Ashley swiveled with her, Ashley looking sick and X looking pissed, "you want two things from me, and I only want one from you."

Out of the corner of my eye I studied some of the other

villains. They looked a little pale. *It could be any of them floating there next to the Countess, I realized. Any of us, I amended.*

"I am a business woman, amongst other things," the Cruel Countess said, "and as a business woman, I'm looking for the most profitable deal. The only time I accept a two-for-one deal is when it is to my advantage. This is not one of those times.

"So," she said, coming to a stop in front of me, "I'm willing to exchange one of my prisoners for you. Either your sister or your ... *lover.*"

Ashley's eyes widened, and she cast a glance over at X before her gaze darted back to me. Even now, with the Cruel Countess a few wrong moves away from killing us all, I could see her judge-y gaze. *Him? Reeeaaally?*

Sister disapproves. Big surprise there.

I focused on the matter at hand. The Cruel Countess wanted to do a hostage exchange, essentially. I'd be stepping in for either my sister or X, and they'd be released.

Hypothetically.

Down here, more than a hundred feet underwater in a supervillain's lair, there was no safety, no true freedom. But more help was on its way.

"You get three seconds," the Countess said, "or else the trade is off."

A no-brainer. "Let go of my sister."

Abruptly, my sister dropped to the floor. I rushed to her. "Ash—"

No sooner had I knelt than I was jerked up into the air. My lips sealed shut, and invisible hands yanked my arms behind my back.

And to think I'd snickered not an hour ago at a hog-tied Chameleon.

My sister stared up at me from the ground, fear written across her tear-tracked face.

"Guards," the Cruel Countess snapped her fingers, "take this one and roughen her up."

My eyes widened, and I tried to shout. Instead, my sealed lips captured the scream. All that came out was a muffled moan. I struggled, just as I'd seen Ashley and X do. No use; the power that bound me didn't give.

"Wait," the Cruel Countess said. She swiveled and headed for the glass wall, dragging X and me with her. She stared into the dark water, forcing me to gaze into it as well. My eyes caught movement. From the murkiness, sharks approached the wall, their movements fluid and somehow sinister.

The Cruel Countess stroked the glass, a smile blooming along her face. The sharks approached her.

A swarm of sharks gathered on the other side of the glass, almost as though summoned by her ...

The Cruel Countess lifted a finger. "Before you're finished with the girl, come get me. I'd like to demonstrate to my guests what a live feeding looks like." She stroked the glass again. "My beasties are hungry."

I started screaming anew, struggling against my invisible binds. It didn't matter that my teammates would find a way in soon. Just the prospect of what the Cruel Countess intended to do to my sister had me breaking out into a cold sweat.

"But what about the other intruders?" someone from the audience asked.

She turned towards the room and eyed them. "You're supervillains. Make yourselves useful and kill them."

CHAPTER 26

Angel

THE CRUEL COUNTESS dragged X and me to a room that branched off the bottom left side of the auditorium.

"So, was it love at first sight?" she asked, tilting her head towards me. "All that muscle and leather—it can take a girl's breath away."

When I just stared at her, she sighed. "I suppose it wouldn't be," she said. "After all, I assume he tried to hurt you, otherwise, you wouldn't have discovered your resilience to his touch."

Crap, she knew that?

"Yes, it makes sense. What doesn't make sense is that you eventually *did* let him get into your pants. I mean, I've heard the rumors that you're loose with men, but there are standards and *there are standards*."

So many reasons to maim this woman; she just added another.

If I looked pissed, X looked murderous. His jaw kept clenching and unclenching, and the muscles of his arms tensed as he strained to free himself.

"But what does that matter?" the Countess said. "Here you both are, a shining example of young love. How romantic."

We arrived in front of a closed door. "You know what's even more romantic than young love? Tragic love.

"Now, you two already have that whole Romeo-and-Juliet thing going on, seeing as how you've come from opposite sides of the justice system, but you haven't yet *died*. Tragically."

The door swung open, and my lungs seized up. All manner of torture devices lined the room—bottomless chairs, chains that dangled from the walls and ceiling, others that locked to the floor. Cuffs with spikes. Dozens of pliers and knives and implements I didn't have names for. Some of the devices looked Medieval, and others, such as the chrome instruments lined on a tray, more modern.

Cruel Countess stepped inside, pulling us along behind her. "Hmmm ..." She tapped her chin. "A little birdy mentioned a theory to me, and now I want to test it."

I was moving again, shifting from the Countess's side to dangle in front of her. She did the same with X, until he and I faced each other.

His eyes searched mine, and I could read anger in them, but also fear. Had the Executioner ever been afraid of anything before this woman?

"Now, that is not the way two lovers interact." The Cruel Countess tsk-ed. "Kiss."

She forced our heads together, and my sealed lips pressed against X's. The action reminded me of when I used to press my Ken and Barbie dolls together as a little girl. Never had I felt more like a toy.

"Okay you two, that's enough." She ripped us away from each other. I swear X trembled with the need to kill this woman.

"Hold hands." One of my arms shot out at the same time X's did, and he clasped my palm.

"X, I think you'll like what's coming next." The Countess smiled to herself.

Phantom claws pressed into my shoulders until the skin broke. With terrible force they dragged down my back, ripping through flesh and muscle. My back arched, my muffled mouth sealing in my scream. I waited for the pain to abate.

But it didn't.

Because X and I are touching. Somehow she discovered all our secrets.

My back felt like Cinder had decided to hold an open flame to it, the pain refusing to lessen. So this was what people normally felt when they were wounded. No wonder so many avoided injury.

X squeezed my hand tightly, and I chanced a glance at him. His normally stoic face was gone. Agony, then wrath, then agony once more flickered across his features. His nostrils flared. *Wrath.*

I felt my cheeks slice open, then my shoulders, down my arms—

A dull thud sounded from somewhere outside the room.

I kneeled over as much as I could, two trails of blood trickling off my boots and onto the ground.

Drip-drip-drip-drip ...

"The little birdy *was* right. How very interesting."

I tried to catch my breath through my nose, my eyes leaking tears from the pain. All the while the Cruel Countess forced X to keep squeezing my hand.

Another thud, closer this time. The Countess frowned but didn't pause from her work.

In the next instant our hands broke apart and I began healing, my body stitching itself back together.

"Now that we've gotten that out of the way, it's time for the main event."

"X, I want you over there." She pointed to the far wall, where chains of all lengths were bolted.

X's body barreled towards it. As soon as his back hit the wall, the chains coiled around his legs, arms and torso, pinning him to it. "For now, you will watch."

The Cruel Countess glanced around the room. Spotting a regular chair, she waved it forward. It scraped across the ground, halting only once it reached us.

"Angel, it's time to make good on your end of the bargain," the Cruel Countess said.

Unless my teammates found us in the next minute, this was it. The Cruel Countess planned on stealing my power here, now.

X renewed his struggles. I could hear his muffled shouts and see the fear that gleamed in his eyes.

"What was that, X? I can't hear you." She smiled and hummed to herself as she forced my body into the chair. Unlike the other torture devices, this one had no straps to hold me in. It didn't need to, not when the Cruel Countess could keep me in place so effectively with her telekinesis.

She leaned over the chair, resting her hands on my forearms, her eyes boring into mine. I'd gotten a good look at my share of criminals, and of them all, her eyes were the deadest.

Her nails bit into my skin and her earlier smile vanished. The cat was almost done toying with its mouse.

"You *stupid* girl. Thinking to evade me. And you," she glared at X, "keeping her from me. Breaking into my sanctuary."

This was her sanctuary? I took a good look at the torture devices and remembered the cells full of broken and battered prisoners. What kind of monster would find this place soothing?

"How dare you defy me," her voice rose, "how dare you cross me. *I* am the closest thing there is to God."

Bitch was cray cray.

That was the only explanation for this nonsense she was now spouting off.

Her nails pierced my skin as she squeezed my arms. "You've both cost me. You've cost me so much."

Distant shouts interrupted the Cruel Countess's tirade. She leaned away from me, trying to hear better.

The sound of footfalls echoed down the corridor, coming towards us.

Boom!

The walls shook.

Hello, Cinder.

The footfalls sounded louder. A second later, a guard in a black uniform skidded to a stop just outside the door, bracing himself against the frame. "Countess," he breathed, "the intruders have killed the guards and taken the blonde prisoner."

My heart soared. That had to be my sister.

I saw the moment the last of the Cruel Countess's control snapped. She threw a blast of wind at the man. "Then go get her!"

The guard fell, then clutched the doorframe to keep from blowing away. "They've breached the cellblock. We— we might not be able to hold them off."

The Cruel Countess shrieked, throwing a blast of fire at the man. He howled as his uniform caught on fire and he rolled, trying to stamp the flames out.

When she rotated back to me, I smiled. Regardless of what happened in this room, my sister would be okay. I could live—or die—with that.

The Cruel Countess looked feral, and at my expression her face contorted further. "You think you've won?" She grabbed my jaw. "*Do you?*"

I stared at her for a long moment. Then I smiled again and nodded.

"Then you're wrong." Without looking away from me, she said, "Say goodbye, X. Your girlfriend is about to die."

THE CRUEL COUNTESS was done playing with us. Now that she was no longer fully in control of the situation, we were a source of anger, not perverse amusement.

I was about to witness firsthand what X had told me.

She steals powers.

Time to see if she could really kill a healer.

She still gripped my jaw, her nails biting into my skin. Jerking my face forward, she pressed her mouth against mine, unsealing my lips. This couldn't be mistaken for a kiss. More like reverse resuscitation; rather than breathing life into me, she wanted to take it from me.

She inhaled. My back arched in pain as she began to rip my power from me, and I screamed into her mouth. It felt as though she shredded through flesh, peeling away the part of me that healed like it were a skin she could wear.

Must get it all. Used to be easier. Swifter.

I blinked as the Cruel Countess's thoughts bubbled up into my head. A barrier broke, and then I didn't know where she ended and I began.

So many faces. Laughing, smiling, now screaming, screaming as I took, took, took from them.

Never enough. I want more. They are all sheep and I will sheer them of their wool. I am the shepherd. I am God.

Holy shit this woman truly is nuts.

Too many. Hard to keep straight. Harder to keep reaping. My power slows. Don't halt! Don't halt! Ate their memories with their abilities. Never bargained for that. Can't stop. Need more.

I WILL RULE THE WORLD.

I kept screaming into her mouth, breaking under the onslaught of so much pain and so many emotions. The more the Cruel Countess siphoned away my power, the more my memories fuzzed out of focus.

Suddenly, the weight that held me in place lifted. Behind me I heard chains fall, clanging against the wall.

The Cruel Countess released my jaw and stumbled back, horror written on her face. "What did you do to me?" she whispered.

I stood, my body free of her hold. I was tired—so, so tired—but now that her power didn't bear down on me, my limbs felt lighter than air. My memories slowly seeped back into focus. I'd come so close to losing them.

I heard ominous footfalls approach me from behind. A moment later, X stepped up to my side. Rage rolled off of him like a storm as he stared down at the Cruel Countess.

She lifted her hand, presumably to use one of her powers, but nothing happened. And I knew why.

She no longer could use any of them. They were gone, gone, gone.

The Cruel Countess stared at her hand as though it betrayed her. In a way, it had.

"What did you do to me?" she repeated, glancing up.

I focused my steely gaze on her. "I healed you."

CHAPTER 27

Angel

WHAT TRUMPS ALL superpowers? Life and death.

The woman in front of me had been sick. Very sick. All those powers had deteriorated the Cruel Countess's body, and they were beginning to claim her mind. My power had eliminated the foreign powers like it would a pathogen.

"No ..." Her voice was a whisper. Her eyes finally filled with emotion. Loss, terror, fear played out in them.

I leaned against the chair I'd been forced to sit in not a minute before.

"You okay?" X asked, never taking his eyes off the Cruel Countess.

"Fine."

X nodded. He stalked past me. Slowly. A wolf circling prey, looking for the right angle to pounce.

His face appeared calm, but his eyes were alight with retribution.

A supervillain will live long enough to carry out a vendetta.

"Two years you've taken from my life. Dozens of supers you let die to feed you. And this is how you end. By my hand." He grabbed the Cruel Countess by the throat.

She began shrieking as his touch burned her from the inside out.

"Executioner ... please," she begged, clawing at his grip on her neck.

He stared her down, his expression morphing into the professional mien he usually wore.

The Cruel Countess made a grab for his face.

"Go ahead," he said, "Try to steal my ability. You already know that it will kill you."

The skin along her right hand began to redden and bubble, and sizzling blood began to leak from her left eye.

Sssss–BOOM! Sssss–BOOM! BOOM! BOOM! BOOM!

I gripped the chair next to me as the earth shook. The bombs went off in quick succession. Who was the idiot that pissed Cinder off?

A groan worked its way through the walls of the lair, the sound sickening. One of the iron bolts in the wall of room screeched.

I caught sight of it just as it turned ever so slightly.

"X," I said, backing away, "we need to go."

"Not until I know she's dead," he ground out.

"X–"

Sssss–BOOM!

With a shriek, the bolt shot out and water hissed through the opening.

Not good, not good, not good.

I was done waiting. "Vengeance will come later." I grabbed his arm and yanked. He lost his hold on the Cruel Countess, and she went tumbling, a mass of shiny blisters peppering her skin.

He glanced at where I touched him, then up at me. "You can still touch me."

I paused, staring at his bare forearm. He was right. His touch didn't hurt. Somehow I still had my power. A riddle to solve later.

A puddle formed at our feet. We needed to get out of here. I gave his arm a tug and we began moving.

I could feel his eyes on me as he followed me out. "Are you really okay?" he asked.

"Fine," I said, my voice breathless as I stumbled onwards.

He let go of my hand. "You're not," X growled.

Sssss–BOOM! Sssss–BOOM!

"Let's worry about that after we get out of here." We still had to grab my sister, free the prisoners, and somehow surface from this subterranean hellhole.

I stopped in front of the doorway to the auditorium.

And take out a bunch of supervillains, I thought, taking in the fighting mass of criminals and heroes.

Cinder appeared at the top of the stairway, several of the prisoners fanning out around her, one of them Ashley.

The tension that had been tightly wound around my core now loosened. There she was. Safe.

Cinder turned to the prisoners. "If any of you have a bone to pick with these assholes," she nodded to the villains currently overtaking the room, "now's you chance." She glanced across the auditorium, and I followed her gaze to a clock.

6:39 a.m.

"You've got ten minutes people," Cinder said, "then we need to book it out of here."

I headed towards the group of released prisoners as they descended the auditorium stairs. Towards my sister.

I saw a blur of movement from my left a split-second before a body collided into me. Viper, a supervillain I only vaguely recognized, pinned me to the ground.

His forked tongue flicking out of his mouth. "Healer meat will taste—"

I drew my arm back and socked him once, twice, three times before he rolled off of me. I stood as he held his head.

"You know that saying about not kicking a horse while it's down?" I said conversationally to X, who now fought another attacker.

X grabbed the man by the scruff, and well, *that* was game over. "What about it?"

"It never said anything about snakes." And then I kicked the man in the head, knocking him out.

When I looked up, freed prisoners had joined the foray, picking out men and women who they must've had some serious beef with. They made the rest of us look like we were having tea parties with our opponents. All that pent up rage and hurt surfaced as they fought. They tore at eyes, noses, fingers, genitalia—all those places that made you cringe.

"Angel!" I glanced up at the sound of my name. A supervillain circled my sister.

I didn't think, I ran, pushing past fighters to reach Ashley. Her attacker closed in on her, grabbing her head on either side, preparing to twist her neck.

Not enough time.

I grabbed one of the throwing stars I'd strapped to my suit an eternity ago. Saying a silent prayer, I hurled it at the supervillain.

It whizzed through the air, shooting between fighting pairs, and thumped into the back of the villain's skull.

He dropped his hold on Ashley, taking a couple steps past her before he fell to his knees and slumped forward.

I dashed across the stage, dodging lighting bolts, arrows, and Cinder's gunpowder explosions to get to her. My feet splashed against the thin sheet of water creeping across the floor.

A supervillain grabbed my collar, hauling me back. Before I could so much as ram my elbow into him, his hold loosened. I didn't look back until I reached the stairs. Once I did, I saw X holding the now-screaming villain. He nodded to me, then returned his attention to his target.

The walls made a sickening groan as I raced the rest of the way up to my sister.

My body felt sluggish as I summited the stairs. The sensation was unfamiliar. Too much power had been drained from me. Couldn't think about that. I had to make the most of the adrenaline pumping through my veins.

"Sis?"

My eyes flicked up, and there was Ashley, looking wide-eyed and lost. We fell together at the same time, our arms wrapping tightly around each other. The Hamilton sisters had always been known for their bear hugs.

The building let out another groan, bringing my attention back to the chaos around us.

Reluctantly I untangled myself from Ashley's embrace, noticing that my touch had managed to heal her wounds, even as more of my energy drained from me.

I swiveled away from her and scanned the auditorium. Bodies littered the ground. I swallowed. So many lost. Mostly villains, but I saw some prisoners among the fallen.

Above them, the clock read 6:47. We had five minutes until we were to meet up with Madman and Zephyr.

That wasn't a whole lot of time. I stuck two fingers into my mouth and whistled. "Time to go!" I yelled to the room.

At my call, many of the prisoners backed toward the stairs, fighting off the last of their opponents. Zeus hurtled lightening bolts and Cinder flicked fireballs at the villains that were halting the prisoner's progress.

Rocket flew over to them and assisted some of the weaker prisoners up the stairs, shoving them down when a labrys flew by.

"Take the freed prisoners to the cave," I said when he passed me. "I'll gather the rest and follow you."

Rocket hesitated. Usually I was the one who led the

injured away, but not today. Today, the fight was personal. However, I did touch the injured as they walked by, noticing that I could only partially heal them, and with each touch, my own strength flagged.

"Sis, aren't you coming?" Ashley asked. She shifted her weight, uncertain whether to stay or go.

"I'll be there in a sec."

Her chin trembled, but then she squared her jaw. "I'm not leaving without you," she said stubbornly.

"Yes, you are." My gaze flicked to Rocket, and he flew over to her, hustling her out of the auditorium. She resisted, her eyes watering as she stared at me.

"You better not die, or I'm going to kick your ass," she said.

"Stop being a bully," I said, smiling in spite of myself. "I'll see you soon." *I hope.*

CHAPTER 28

Angel

WHEN MY ATTENTION returned to room, the superheroes still grappled with the enemy, but we were winning. My eyes searched for X. When I caught sight of him, I breathed out a sigh of relief, but only for a moment. He stalked towards the door leading to the torture chamber.

A monster leaned against the doorway, wearing a crimson gown. My mind wouldn't believe this melted, blistered thing had once been the Cruel Countess.

X closed in on her, and I could read the cold purpose in every line of his body.

Behind him, the villain Zeus fought with lifted into the air. A lighting bolt grew in Zeus's hand as he tracked her. Pulling back his arm, Zeus threw his electric javelin. It

should've hit his opponent's chest, but the woman abruptly changed course, and the bolt traveled on, crashing into
the glass window with a loud clap of thunder.

The walls shrieked, the sound thick and terrible.

Cinder threw a fireball at Zeus's opponent, and the
woman fell to the floor in a fiery blaze. "Retreat!" she
cried.

My eyes darted to X, who now circled the Cruel Countess. She, in turn, circled him. Another, softer creak echoed
through the building.

I took a step forward. "X!" I yelled from the top of the
stairs.

The glass wall cracked, the rip heading straight down
the middle of the pane before spider-webbing out. Cinder
and Zeus hauled ass up the stairs, raining down fire and
lightening at the supervillains who tried to follow.

"X!" I screamed again, descending the steps.

X caught sight of me. "Run!" he shouted, his eyes wild.

Zeus caught me around the waist hauling me up with
him.

"Put me down." I struggled against him. "Please, Zeus.
Put me—"

With a final creak, the glass wall shattered, blowing in-
wards. And then the ocean poured in.

"NOOO!" I screamed as the water engulfed both X and
the Cruel Countess.

I was imagining things. The two most powerful supervillains couldn't just be gone.

My X couldn't be gone.

Zeus kept his hold on me as he sprinted up the rest of

the stairs.

"Shit, shit, shit!" Cinder shouted as the water ate up the room below us.

"If I put you down, will you run?" Zeus shouted over the roar of water.

My eyes searched and searched the churning liquid. No X.

"Angel." Zeus shook me lightly.

If I tried to stay behind, Zeus and Cinder would come after me. I'd kill us all. But to leave X behind …

I swallowed and nodded to Zeus. "Yes," I agreed.

My heart ripped. I didn't even know it had carved out a place for X. And if it was anything like the rest of me at the moment, it wasn't going to heal any time soon.

Zeus set me on the ground, and the three of us ran. Along the cellblock blackened doors hung off their hinges. That explained the explosions X and I heard.

X …

I pushed down the rising ache.

Our shoes slapped against the tile. The roar of the ocean sounded behind us, and the lights flickered.

I pumped my arms and legs. Above me, a pipe hissed, and water sprayed across my body.

We left the prison block and passed through the laboratory with its bloody implements. Never again would those tools be used to torture. I had to remember that—that the greater good was served today by eradicating this place.

Seawater rushed down the hallway, quickly surpassing us. It whooshed across the floor, leading us to the next corridor. For several seconds it was a puddle. Then it hit our ankles.

We turned the corner, darting past the row of lockers. X's equipment swirled in the water, a grim reminder of the man I'd left behind.

We slogged through the exit—which had been soldered off its hinges—and into the cave. There Rocket and the rest of the prisoners waited, cold and shivering. Among them was my sister. She visibly relaxed when she caught sight of me.

The water spilled into the cave from the hallway we just left, splashing against the rocks.

I heaved in great lungfuls of air, gasping. It was a feat keeping my legs locked in place when every nerve ending screamed at me to run back inside and retrieve X.

Cinder grabbed my upper arm. "Steady," she said. I could see the warning in her eyes. *Don't even think about it,* they seemed to say.

A loud *thunk* sounded above us where *Dolly Parton* must've landed.

"Let's go, let's go!" Rocket shouted.

Cinder squeezed my arm. "We need to get these men and women onto the boat before Zephyr's wind gives out. Can you do that?"

I nodded rapidly. *Help the prisoners. Save what lives you can.*

And I did, I helped my teammates evacuate each and every one of them, all the while hoping the X would find his way back to the cave. But he never did, and eventually I had no choice but to join the others in the boat and leave the Cruel Countess's lair to its watery grave.

Defeat was a bitter, bitter taste in my mouth. I'd never truly lost anything I cared about.

And now I had.

CHAPTER 29
Two Weeks Later

Angel

"... SO FAR, *twelve bodies have been recovered from the Cruel Countess's Caribbean fortress, where a grizzly showdown claimed the lives of many of the world's top heroes and villains. The Cruel Countess is noticeably not among the fallen, though it's unclear whether she's still at large.*"

Plopping down on the couch with my carton of mint chip ice cream, I grabbed the remote control and clicked off the T.V. The news had been playing around the clock at Madcap Mansion. I couldn't stand it anymore.

I made a promise I'd get everyone out of that lair, and I broke it.

Shadow appeared next to me, spoon in her hand. "Hey girl hey," she said, "care to share?"

"Sure," I said. When I made no move to take the carton's lid off, she did it for me. She swiped herself a spoonful of the mint chip ice cream.

When I didn't follow, she eyed me, then the carton, then me again. "Angel, you need to eat. Remember what the doctor said?"

"Not really," I mumbled.

I did, in fact, remember what the doctor said. My power remained, but it had been weakened by the exchange with the Cruel Countess. I would fully recover, but rest and over-eating were required. Apparently the more calories I ate, the faster they could be turned to energy that would strengthen my power.

Until I was back to full health, I wasn't allowed to save lives. Not even the occasional hospital drop-in. My teammates had gone so far as to hide their dying houseplants from me. Assholes.

"Is this about the Executioner?" Shadow asked.

My throat tightened.

X probably died in that lair. The absence of a body didn't mean he was alive. I drew in a shaky breath.

"Dude," Shadow swiped another scoopful of ice cream, "that totally sucks. I mean, falling in love is hard enough for us as is, but a supervillain ... and then he has the audacity to die on you." She shook her head and licked her spoon. "Bet he banged like a god."

I could feel fat tears prepping themselves to roll down my cheeks. Since when did I indulge in pity parties? Never!

Zephyr wandered into the living room, her face lighting

up when she saw us. "I heard a rumor that ice cream and my favorite girls were out here. Good to know the rumor proved true." She plopped down on my other side.

Leaning over me, she grabbed my untouched spoon and scooped out some ice cream. "Keep this appetite up Angel and maybe you can save a woodland creature in another year."

"Zeph," Shadow chastised, "be realistic. It'll take her six months, tops."

"You two suck at cheering me up." Eating my ice cream and making fun of me. In their defense, this tactic had worked in the past.

"Yeah, well, Madman told me you were sucking something else while running with the Executioner." Zephyr waggled her eyebrows.

Shadow had already scooped ice cream onto her spoon when I snatched the piece of silverware out of her hand. I pulled the tip of the utensil back and shot the ice cream at Zephyr. The blob of mint chip beaned her right between the eyes.

"You little skank!" she shouted. A second later she shoved her spoonful of ice cream up my nose.

I let out a shocked, nasally laugh as it dripped down my upper lip.

Shadow snatched the carton out of my hands and sprinted away, cackling, "Mine, all mine!"

"That sneaky bitch ..." Zephyr muttered, chasing after her.

I held my hand below my chin. I needed a napkin, then a shower. Once those were out of the way, I'd plot my revenge.

Cinder sashayed by. "Hey Angel," she said, eyeing the pale green ice cream dripping down my face, "package came for you. It's in your room."

"Thanks."

I headed into the kitchen and wiped off the sticky remnants of ice cream. Cupping water from the faucet, I splashed it against my face until I was sure I'd gotten it all off.

For a brief moment there, I'd felt carefree, and it reminded me of the old Angel, the mindlessly happy one. Back then no one had knocked down my boundaries and weaseled their way into my heart. I wanted that lightness again.

Not going to get it back for a while. Maybe ever.

I wiped my chin off and headed for my room.

The hallway was quiet, but then again, it was evening. Most of my housemates were on duty, patrolling the streets of L.A. Lucky ducks. At least they had work to distract them. Meanwhile all I had were endless hours of wallowing.

And there was Chub-Chub. But even he had almost died on me. I'd found him swimming sideways when I returned from Miami. I had to touch his little body to bring him back from the edge.

I stepped into my room and froze. All thoughts of my fish fled as I stared into the darkness. There, waiting for me, was the Executioner.

CHAPTER 30

Angel

I MADE A small, embarrassing sound, and then I tackle-hugged X.

His arms clasped me tightly, like I was the one that might suddenly disappear. In the past, he'd been hesitant about touching me. Now he wasn't; he knew exactly where he wanted his hands to be.

X nuzzled my face, pressing his lips to the shell of my ear. I could feel his smile in the kiss.

"You're happy to see me." He sounded surprised.

He's alive, he's alive—he's alive.

He'd survived the Cruel Countess, escaped the cave-in, and led me to believe he was dead for two entire weeks.

I breathed the smell of him. "You *bastard*." My voice

came out as a choked sob. "I thought you *died*." Two stupid tears leaked from my eyes.

X leaned away from me, his grip moving from my back to my neck. He tilted my head up, frowning at my tears. "You missed me?"

I shoved him hard enough for him to stumble back. "What do you think?"

He stared me down, looking too gorgeous for words. His leather jacket fit him like sin, and his hood was down, showing off those dark, glittering eyes. He'd tied his hair back, away from his face.

I could lose myself memorizing every detail of this man.

"I think I missed you more," he said.

X closed the distance between us in two steps, and then he kissed me fiercely.

My heart! Never had it felt such lows, and never had it soared so high.

I clung to X's forearms as my lips moved against his and reveled in the taste of him. His mouth and his embrace were both warm, comforting—the exact opposite of what one would expect. And his touch ... even in my weakened state I was immune to his punishing ability.

He's alive and he came back for me.

I broke away. "How did you escape?"

His breath came out in pants, and he gazed at my mouth longingly. "After the window broke, the water swept me up and dragged me to a stairwell that led to the fortress's docking bay. I managed to board one of the submarines the Cruel Countess kept there, said a prayer, and evacuated the place."

X rubbed a thumb over my lower lip. "You were worried?" He kept asking these questions like he needed reassurance.

"Of course," I whispered.

He smiled at that, staring at my mouth. "I don't know if anyone's ever worried for me before."

"Get used to it."

Hope bloomed in his eyes.

"What happened to the Cruel Countess?" I asked.

His expression turned grim. "I don't know. The water separated us."

She could still be out there, disfigured and stripped of her stolen powers, but alive nonetheless. If that was the case, I was sure I'd see her again.

I'd be ready.

X's fingers moved to my neck and absently stroked the skin there. I wanted to stretch out and let him pet the rest of me.

Soon, I reassured myself.

"Where have you been since you escaped?" *Why didn't you come for me earlier?*

I think X understood my unspoken question because he searched my eyes, surprised—and, from what I could tell, delighted—by my interest in him. "I had to tie up the last of my business and exact my retribution before I could come to you."

Exact his retribution? I didn't want to know.

"Wait," I narrowed my eyes, "why couldn't you visit me first?"

"Because I didn't want to return to you a criminal."

I tilted my head at his words. "What do you mean?" He couldn't be saying what I thought he was.

Could he?

"I've received a pardon of sorts. I'm no longer wanted—in the U.S. I'm still working on the other countries."

My eyes bugged out. "How?" Our government had a massive hate-on for this guy.

"Money. Favors. The usual." He sounded so bored.

"And it worked?"

X picked up an empty Cup of Soup sitting on my dresser. "It did."

He set the Styrofoam cup down and fingered the Gatorade bottle next to it. "You've been sick." Not a question.

"I'm still recovering from the Cruel Countess."

His brows slammed down. "Who's been taking care of you?" he asked, like I had a slew of servants waiting to heal me. I supposed that to a supervillain, healing as many people as I had earned me some reciprocation.

If only.

I lifted a shoulder and dropped it. "Me."

He touched my cheek. "Not anymore, Angel."

The corner of my mouth lifted. "You're going to nurse me back to health?"

"I am."

X grabbed Chub-Chub's bowl off my bureau. "Get what you need; I'm not letting you go until you've recovered your strength."

Oh goody, another kidnapping session. Not that he'd have to drag me away this time.

"Do you even know what nursing me back to health

entails?"

X raised an eyebrow and glanced around the room, his eyes landing on the empty cartons of ice cream, the numerous energy bar wrappers, and the horde of Girl Scout cookies Zephyr had bought me earlier.

"Well, for one," he said, "it appears you require an on-hand grocery store. For another, I know that sick people have to stay in bed. Conserve energy. I'll be enforcing that rule starting now."

X handed me my fishbowl, then scooped me up into his arms. I yelped. He began walking us to my open window.

"Wait!" I protested.

X halted. "Do you want me to leave without you?" he asked, his brow furrowing.

No. Not at all. Please don't leave me again.

"I will, if that's what you want," he insisted. He searched my eyes. "I might no longer be a wanted supervillain, but my life's not easy. You—" He hesitated before continuing on. "You don't have to be a part of it."

The Executioner was giving me an out. How very ... selfless of him.

Something close to panic rose within me. To find out he survived only to have him exit my life again. I'd hunt him down like the Cruel Countess did me if he decided to disappear.

"I want to go with you. I just ... I also want my clothes, and my make-up, and my favorite movies, and my laptop, and my phone."

He stared at me, a smile slowly blooming along his face. I saw hope flicker in his eyes again. "Good. I'll provide you your amenities ... eventually."

"Eventually?" I said, raising my eyebrows. "I don't think so."

"Fine," he conceded, the smile continuing to tease his lips. "I'll come back for them as soon as I put you in the car."

He resumed carrying me, which was utterly ridiculous, but hey, I'd enjoy the free ride.

"Do you remember how I told you that supervillains will live long enough to see their vendettas through?" X asked conversationally.

I hugged Chub-Chub's bowl to me. "What about it?"

His voice dropped low. "You tied me to my own bed. I plan on returning the favor."

Heat pooled in my core. "You're going to shackle me to your bed?" I tried to keep the excitement from my voice but failed miserably.

"I'm going to do that and so much more." A threat—or a promise, depending on how you looked at it.

A normal person would be scared. But I wasn't normal. I ate calamity for breakfast. I healed the sick, took down supervillains, and fell for a man whose touch could kill.

I was the furthest thing from normal.

"You better watch your back, X," I said. "You're not the only one with vendettas."

"Oh, coming to the dark side?"

A hero and a villain met, once upon a time. Mortal enemies. And then the impossible happened. A touch, a kiss, a whole lot of fighting ... and then this.

I smiled up at X. "No, just meeting you somewhere in the middle."

Other books by Laura Thalassa

The Unearthly Series:
The Unearthly
The Coveted
The Cursed
The Forsaken
The Damned

The Fallen World Series:
The Queen of All that Dies
The Queen of Traitors

The Vanishing Girl Series:
The Vanishing Girl
The Decaying Empire

Novellas:
Reaping Angels

BORN AND RAISED in Fresno, California, Laura Thalassa spent her childhood reading and creating fantastic tales. She now spends her days penning everything from young adult paranormal romance to new-adult dystopian novels. Thalassa lives with her husband and partner in crime, Dan Rix, in Oakhurst, California. For more information, please visit laurathalassa.blogspot.com.